Loved by the Mafia Underboss

Moscatelli Crime Family Book 2

By Cameron Hart

CONNECT WITH ME!

For more info on upcoming books, sneak previews of new projects, and to sign up for my newsletter, make sure to check out my website: cameronhart.net.

Find me on Facebook (facebook.com/cameronhartauthor/) and Instagram (@cameron.hart.author)!

Receive FREE copies of my new books before they hit Amazon by becoming an ARC reader. Sign up on my website!

Chapter 1

Luca

I can hear her voice echo throughout the otherwise silent library. The guy at the front desk murmurs something to her in a respectable, quiet tone, and then the insufferable red-headed troublemaker thanks him loudly. Her heels clack deafeningly on the marble floor of the Harold Washington Library Center, where Matteo and Darlene are preparing the rehearsal for their big day tomorrow.

I still can't believe Matteo is getting married. Not only is he the head of the Moscatelli crime family, but he's my best friend. Not that we call each other that or talk about it at all. But it's true all the same.

While he's still a formidable man who commands the armies of the underworld, he now has a softer side to him, one he reserves only for Darlene. Matteo's woman is lovely and a sweetheart who can also slay dragons. She's perfect for Matteo, however unlikely their relationship might be.

Darlene's best friend, however, is not so sweet. Beautiful, yes. But sweet? Fuck no.

"Leena!" The devil herself bursts through the closed doors of the reserved room and runs as fast as her kitten heels will allow. "I'm so sorry I'm late. I swear I left my apartment on time, but then this guy ahead of me in the Starbucks line took *for-fucking-ever* to order his white chocolate, half-caff, almond milk latte with whipped cream. I even aggressively tapped my foot and sighed loudly and everything!" She takes a breath after her long-winded explanation.

"Did you try turning around and leaving without getting your coffee?" I grumble quietly to myself.

The frazzled, hot mess of a woman turns towards me, searing me with her green eyes. Shit. Apparently I wasn't quiet enough.

Freya grins at me like she always does. It annoys me to no end that she's not intimidated by me in the least. As the underboss of the Moscatelli family, I command the attention, respect, and often the fear of everyone around me. So why does Freya find me to be such a great source of entertainment?

Darlene gets Freya's fleeting attention once again and tells her what she's missed. Freya pivots and makes her way towards me.

Freya is a short little thing with curves for days. She's like a fifties pinup, complete with bright frilly dresses, a handkerchief wrapped around her hair, and heels. If you passed her on the street, you might mistake her for a pretty, naive, but endearing twenty-something with a charming smile. But you would be wrong.

4

Once she opens her pouty, bright red lips, it's clear that Freya only knows how to speak in sarcasm and biting remarks. That is, unless she's trying to manipulate me or otherwise mess with me. Her defiant personality is surprisingly large, considering the small package all that fury is wrapped up in.

"I just heard the good news!" Freya says, plopping down next to me on one of the folding chairs set up in the room. I ignore her bright, bubbly voice and her lavender and saltwater scent. "Well? Aren't you going to ask me what the news is?"

Obviously, I'm not.

Freya sighs and smooths out the flowing skirt of her green sundress that hits right above her knees. Not that I'm looking or anything. "Since I know you're dying of curiosity over there but are too stubborn to admit it, I'll just tell you. We're paired up for the walk back down the aisle!"

"Wonderful," I deadpan.

Freya snorts and then swats me on the chest. I bristle at that. No one, fucking *no one*, touches me. And yet, here she is, hitting me right in my goddamn chest. And I just...let her.

"I know you don't hate me as much as you try to pretend."

Once again, I ignore her. She's right, of course. I don't hate her. I don't know how I feel about the fiery woman next to me with all the subtlety of an avalanche.

She's flighty, exasperating, and sometimes downright aggressive. Freya is a force to be reckoned with, that's for sure.

The only time I've seen her quiet and well-behaved was when Darlene was kidnapped. Freya somehow channeled her chaotic energy into not only tracking down Darlene's whereabouts, but getting ahold of my number as well. I've yet to figure out how the fuck she pulled that off.

Freya had called me and let Matteo and I know where Darlene was being held. She even had the audacity to go there by her own damn self before giving us a call. Irresponsible, thoughtless woman. I had to respect her tenacity, though. She wanted to lead the charge, but when she saw Matteo had brought a veritable army of men who were armed to the teeth, Freya backed down.

As a rule, Matteo and I never enter a potentially hostile situation together, let alone a situation we know will result in gunfire and lives lost. As his number two, I'm usually in those positions myself while he makes the calls. This was Darlene, however, so of course he was going to be there. Which meant I had to hang back. With Freya.

I remember the shell of a woman I had begrudgingly started to get to know over the previous weeks via supervised phone calls Darlene had with Freya. Something about seeing the power of the Moscatelli family in full force must have made everything come into focus for her. Darlene was in serious shit.

Freya's light dimmed, her shoulders drooped, and she wrapped her arms around herself. She looked so damn vulnerable. Not that I noticed. I had unnamed feelings about her then, too, but I pushed them so far down, I'm sure they will never see the light of day.

Why then, do they keep cropping up here and there? I'll catch sight of her in the library with the sunlight shining on her bright red curls, making them glow. Or I'll hear her throaty laugh, followed by an unladylike snort. Sometimes I even see her give Darlene a rare hug, letting her tough, give-no-shits attitude go for a brief moment of vulnerability. Each of these little moments tug at something in my chest, making it looser, breaking me apart in a way that makes me uncomfortable.

"Stop daydreaming about me!" Freya breaks into my thoughts. I grunt at her, not liking how close she is to the truth. "You gotta go stand up there now. But don't you go missing me. I'll be there soon enough."

She gives me a saccharine smile and bats her long eyelashes at me. The little brat.

I make my way up to the front of the room and take my place next to Matteo. He nods at me, silently thanking me for showing my support. We've known each other for more than half our lives, and we've been the top two men in the family for a decade. Matteo and I don't need words to show gratitude, and we sure as fuck don't need hugs like Freya and Darlene do.

I avoid looking at the curvy woman in the green dress with red, wavy hair flowing down her back as she makes her way down the aisle. Or, I try to, but my eyes don't seem to be getting the message. Just when I think Freya is about to walk right up to me, she winks and then kisses Darlene on the forehead.

I didn't even notice Darlene was walking down the aisle with Freya, although it makes sense. These two are each other's only family, even if they aren't related by blood.

Freya must be walking Darlene down the aisle in place of a father figure. My chest gets tight with that uncomfortable, unidentified feeling again when I think about Freya not having any family.

We stand on the makeshift stage while the priest walks us through how the ceremony will proceed. He answers a few questions and confirms the number of guests, the seating arrangements, and blah, blah, blah.

Darlene and Matteo kiss briefly and then head down the aisle, arm in arm, with a smile of genuine love on their faces. I can't say I've ever seen that look directed at me, and I've certainly never had that look myself. I wonder what it's like.

"Psst," Freya whispers. Or, I think it's supposed to be a whisper, but it's somehow louder than her normal voice. "We're up!"

I sigh and start walking back down the aisle. Freya sprints to keep up, and then she does something totally unprecedented. She loops her arm through mine.

I freeze and stare down at where we're touching. I feel the warmth of her skin spread throughout my body and sink into my goddamn bones. It's too much. Not enough.

"No one touches me," I grit out, trying to yank my arm away from her grasp. She just squeezes me tighter and leans in closer, so her body brushes up against mine.

"Lucky me, then," Freya teases, dragging me along towards the back door of the room. I have no choice but to stumble after her, wondering what the actual fuck just happened.

"Freya, you'll be riding with Luca to the rehearsal dinner," Darlene says sweetly. I notice she didn't ask, nor did she direct her words at me.

I roll my eyes, but then catch Matteo glaring at me. That look says it all. A directive from Darlene is the same as a directive from Matteo himself, so I better shut up and do whatever the hell she says, especially since it's her wedding.

Normally I prefer to drive myself, especially after Matteo's long-time driver, Tony, betrayed the family and hand-delivered Darlene to the enemy. However, events such as these – even the *rehearsal* for events like these, demand a show of power and wealth. Thus, most of us have drivers carting us around in lavish vehicles from point A to point B.

I slip into the back seat of the latest model Lincoln Navigator, wincing as Freya bounces in next to me and slams her door shut. She starts fidgeting immediately, which shouldn't come as a surprise. The woman is incapable of sitting still.

Freya leans forward and rests one elbow on the back of the driver's seat and the other on the back of the passenger's seat before craning her neck even further forward so she can talk to the driver.

"Hi!" She says enthusiastically. The old man jumps in his seat but otherwise doesn't acknowledge her. It seems he and I have a similar reaction to Hurricane Freya. "Could you turn the radio on? 102.7, please!" When she's met with silence, Freya tries again. "It's urban adult contemporary," she adds as if that helps anything.

"What the fuck is urban adult contemporary?" I grumble.

She turns her head to look at me over her shoulder, and I have to look away. I can still feel her touch echoing throughout my body. No need to add her emerald green eyes into the already confusing mix of feelings settling like a boulder on my chest.

I see her shrug out of the corner of my eye. "I don't know. That's just what they say. *'Today's best urban adult contemporary only on 102.7!'*" She says in what I'm assuming is her version of an annoying radio DJ. When no one responds to her, she lets out a dramatic sigh. "*Fiiiiiine.* KISS FM it is. I never took you for a top forty guy, Luca."

"Sit back and put your damn seatbelt on," I growl.

Her eyes go wide and then she narrows them at me, the little green slits of her irises peeking out just enough to let me know she's likely plotting the easiest way to get rid of my body. I hold her gaze and set my jaw, not backing down from my command.

Freya huffs indignantly, but finally sits in her seat properly and clicks her seatbelt into place. "Yes, sir," she mumbles, crossing her arms over her chest like a petulant child.

Well, fuck. Why did that one word go straight to my dick?

I wipe my hands down my face and take a deep breath. It's going to be a long fucking night.

Chapter 2

Freya

It takes monumental effort not to crack a grin at Luca's over the top reaction. He's so fucking *serious* all the time. And quiet. And broody. And boy does he find me infuriating. I love it. I've become quite the expert in how to annoy Luca.

He doesn't like it when I chew my gum loudly and blow huge bubbles. He doesn't like it when I take my shoes off and run through the ridiculous mansion to find Darlene. He doesn't like it when I shout across the library or blast my music and attempt to rap along with Cardi B. In fact, he doesn't seem to like it when I make any noise at all. Which only makes me want to be louder.

"So, what's it like being in the mafia?" I ask sweetly while studying my nails. I really should get a manicure. My cuticles are out of control. Luca doesn't answer, of course, but I hear him sigh. "You're the underboss, which is basically the vice president, right?"

"No," he mumbles. "It's not like the vice president."

God, his voice. It's like honey over gravel. Smooth, with an undertone of grit and determination. Despite my teasing him endlessly and trying to get a reaction out of him, I do recognize that he's a very powerful man. It's in his voice and the way he carries himself. Luca exudes authority and his mere presence commands respect.

In other words, his ego can afford to be brought down a peg or two. Or five.

"What's it like, then?" Unsurprisingly, he doesn't answer. "Fine. I'll tell you about my latest job. I'm working in a little shop in Water Tower Place that sells lotions, candles, and bath bombs." Luca raises one eyebrow slightly, which is pretty much the most positive reaction I've ever gotten out of him. "Not *those* kinds of bombs. Not everything is life and death, you know. Some people just want to take a bath and throw a little scented, soapy, fizzy ball in the water. It's not really my thing, but they are pretty popular."

Luca hums in acknowledgment. Hey, that's a step up from grunting.

"I think I'm going to quit after the wedding, though. I know what you're thinking. *Really, Freya? You're quitting yet another job?* To that, I say, hell yes. Why would I limit myself to only having one experience, you know? Life is for living and I want to have as many different experiences as I can."

After a brief pause to make sure he's still listening, I continue. "Plus, a lady walked in yesterday and yelled at me because one of the bath bombs she bought turned her blue and she wanted her money back *and* five hundred dollars for her distress. Can you believe that bullshit? The refund, sure, but five hundred dollars? She was rude as fuck. I may have told her that. It's possible I also told her I didn't see any evidence of blue stains on her skin. Anyway. I might be fired when I go back for my shift in a few days. But that's how these things go, right?

"I'm thinking I should try a cleaning lady gig next. You know, like one of those people who go in and clean huge offices after everyone has gone home for the night? I think it'd be perfect. I could make a whole cleaning playlist and then sing along while scrubbing the floors or whatever."

I fold my hands in my lap and turn to look at Luca, who is pretending not to notice me. "Okay. I told you about me and my career and aspirations. Now you go."

Luca looks at his watch and grumbles something about wishing they had chosen a closer restaurant. God, he's adorable.

"I deal with daily operations and I oversee the capos."

"So, you're like a regional manager?"

He scoffs and growls about how I'm insufferable. I can't contain my grin.

"Careful, little girl," he warns.

Holy shit. I've never heard that tone from him. Deep. Dark. Dangerous. Those three words wrap around my body like a silk rope, tightening around my lower stomach and creating intense pressure. Damn him and the way my body reacts to every single thing he does.

I clear my throat and look away from him, trying to keep some sort of composure. "Looks like we're here!" I say with far more enthusiasm than the situation calls for. Luca winces, which makes me smile. "Good talk, Luca. I think it was one of our best ones so far."

He presses his lips in a straight line and clenches his jaw. I know it's probably to hold in whatever snide remark is on the tip of his tongue, but I hope it's partially to hold back a smile. That's my ultimate goal. It's fun to push his buttons, but what I really want is for him to chill the fuck out and smile. Hell, I'd take a smirk. Anything, really.

Then again, I don't know if I can handle his smile. Will his blue eyes sparkle? Will his sharp, angular features soften a bit? Will his lips simply turn up at the ends, or will he part them and show off his white teeth?

Just thinking about it has my cheeks heating up. There's no denying that Luca is a Greek god walking amongst us mere mortals. Again, all the more reason to take a stab at those impenetrable walls of his.

The driver opens my door, which pulls me back into the moment. Luca is standing in front of the door to the restaurant, holding it open for me. I've never seen him act so well-behaved and polite before. I can't help but smirk and raise an eyebrow at him as I walk inside.

When we get to the private room in the back of the restaurant, which is one of many owned by the Moscatelli family, I see there is assigned seating. Guess who I'm sitting next to?

Luca notices at the same time I do. I can tell because he sighs defeatedly.

"Oh, come on. I'm not *that* bad. You can tell me more about being the regional manager of a crime family. I've had some nasty customers, as I've already told you, but I bet you deal with far worse. We can trade war stories."

He doesn't say anything, but to my absolute shock, he pulls my chair out for me. I look up at him questioningly, but he's as stoic as ever. I've never had anyone do this for me, so I'm not quite sure how it works. Do I sit down and then he pushes the chair in? I'm not a small, dainty girl, and I feel like that wouldn't work so well. Am I supposed to start sitting and he pushes the chair in to catch me before I fall flat on my butt? That requires a level of trust I've only ever given Leena.

"Stop overthinking and sit your ass down."

My body responds to his command before my brain even processes his words. Before I know it, I'm sitting at the table. What the hell? Luca bossed me around and I just...obeyed?

He takes his seat next to me and busies himself with looking over the menu. I just sit there and study him, trying to figure out how he moved my body without even touching me. No one, and I mean *no one,* tells me what to do. Not anymore. Not ever again.

Was it that tone of voice? The dark, silky one from earlier? Was it his leather and whiskey scent that I can't seem to get out of my nostrils? I smell him now as he sits next to me. Why does it remind me of home? It makes no sense. I've never had a home, so how can this man make me nostalgic for something that doesn't exist?

Darlene and Matteo enter the room and stand at the head of the long table where we are sitting. They give some speech about appreciating us, and I know it was one-hundred percent Darlene's idea to thank people in the wedding party. That girl. Sweet as pie, yet totally badass.

My mind wanders to that horrible night she was kidnapped. I was out of my mind with worry. It physically hurt me to not rush into the abandoned building where the Ricci's were holding her captive. But I only had a small pistol in my purse, which wouldn't do much damage against dozens of armed mafia soldiers.

Luca stayed with me while we watched Matteo's men infiltrate the building. He stood by me when the first shot rang out, followed by multiple shots, and then full-on rapid fire. He didn't say anything, didn't comfort me, didn't offer a shoulder to cry on. But his calming, commanding presence grounded me just enough to hang on to my last thread of sanity.

I steal another glance at Luca. Even now, he exudes a quiet strength and confidence I don't understand. Even when I annoy him and get him all riled up, he never truly breaks. He never cracks. He never yells or threatens or lays a hand on me. It's more than I can say for other dominating men I've come across in my life.

Holy shit. Is that why I do it? Because I want to see how far I can push him? See if he'd ever hurt me? Why would that even matter?

You're trying to see if he can handle you. All of you.

Nope. Too far, inner monologue. I don't want to be handled. I'm my own damn woman and fuck anyone who says otherwise. And yet...

"Excuse me," I murmur before leaving my seat and heading towards the bathroom. I just need a moment to rein in my intrusive, unwelcome thoughts.

Once inside the bathroom, I take a few calming breaths and then grab a paper towel and wet it down before dabbing it on my face and the back of my neck. When I've finally managed to control my breathing and regulate my body temperature, I stare at myself in the mirror, preparing for a good old-fashioned pep talk.

"Listen here, bitch. You don't need a man. Luca is fun to annoy and that's it. Leena deserves a happily ever after, but you don't. And even if you did, why are you hung up on Luca? Get your shit together. For Leena and Matteo. Just get through tomorrow."

I feel my nails bite into my palms, but I don't unclench my fists. That little spark of pain is enough to pull me back into the moment. It's a habit of mine. I'm not sure where I picked it up, but I pretty much always have little half-moon marks on my palms from digging my fingernails into my skin. Just one more fucked up thing about me.

Taking a deep breath, I shake my hands out and exit the bathroom.

A shadow catches my eye when I step out of the bathroom. There's a man standing at the end of the hallway; with the way his suit jacket is flipped open, I can see he has a gun. There isn't much lighting in the hallway, so I can't make out his face before he turns the corner and slips away from me.

I don't realize I'm shaking until I stumble backward and lean against the wall. I remind myself this is the rehearsal dinner for the head of the mafia. Of course, there will be men in suits with guns. I should be used to it by now.

My brain is on board with my explanation of the strange man, but my heart is rattling around painfully inside my ribcage and I can't seem to get enough oxygen into my lungs.

There's no one coming after you. It's been years. And they don't know what you look like. It's fine. You're fine. You're a badass, now act like it!

Ah, yes. There's an inner monologue I can work with.

I smooth down my dress and take a few unsteady steps before finding my rhythm and confidence again. By the time I get back to my seat, I'm mostly recovered.

That is, until Luca looks at me with what could possibly be described as concern. But that can't be right. Whatever look he's giving me is turning my insides to mush. My eyes are burning with...tears? Fuck that noise.

I turn away from the tall, muscled mountain of a man and his prying, all-knowing eyes, focusing instead on my water glass. It's suddenly the most interesting thing in the world. I reach out for it, grasping the glass in my hand. The cold condensation on the outside feels good on the skin of my palm, which is irritated from my nervous habit.

Water spills over the rim when I lift it up. I'm shaking. Goddamnit. I set the glass down and withdraw my hand, placing it in my lap. I didn't think I could still be rattled this badly from one little scare. And it wasn't even a real scare, it was just my dumb brain filling in details that weren't even there. I'm fine. I'm fucking *fine*.

"Everything okay?" Luca's voice is soft and uncharacteristically gentle.

Something about that has all of my defenses rising to the surface. I don't just have walls around my heart, I have a fortress complete with snipers, barbed wire fences, and savage dogs with a taste for blood.

"I'm fine," I spit out. "Maybe if I had better company I wouldn't have to hide out in the bathroom."

Instead of sighing or growling at me, Luca just continues to stare. He's taking me in, all of me. It shouldn't make me feel vulnerable, what with the barbed wire fences around my heart and all, but there's something about those steel blue eyes that get to me.

Luca is trying to figure me out, and I don't like it. He's trying to see past my obnoxious exterior and learn what makes me tick. What makes me scared. What makes me...me. No one has ever cared enough to try to know me like that. No one except Leena.

I'm not sure exactly what he's looking for, or what he's finding for that matter. When he eventually tears his eyes away from mine, I feel like he took a piece of me with him.

I thought this night would be a fun way to mess with Luca, but it appears that he's the one messing with me.

Chapter 3

Luca

It's the morning of Darlene and Matteo's wedding, and I've been assigned to Freya duty. My orders from the boss are to make sure she gets to the library in one piece, with plenty of time to get Darlene and herself ready for the big day.

I had no idea what all went into planning a wedding, but now I know more than I ever thought I would. It's not something I've ever considered for myself. Marriage, that is. I'm not that guy. I didn't think Matteo was that guy either, but clearly he's turned over a new leaf. I wonder what it would be like to find a woman who has the power to actually change who you are for the better.

Shaking those thoughts from my head, I pull into the parking lot of Freya's apartment building. I frown when I notice there aren't many security measures. The building itself isn't the worst I've seen, but you don't even have to walk inside the building to get to the apartments, seeing as the front doors all face the outside. Why it bothers me so much to see Freya living here, I have no idea.

I'm about to check the text Matteo sent me with Freya's apartment number, but then I hear her. She's singing, if you can call it that, at the top of her lungs. Screeching is more like it. To be fair, the musician she's trying to sing along with is also screeching. It seems Freya's taste in music is much like the rest of her – obnoxious just for the sake of being obnoxious.

Taking a deep breath, I raise my hand and knock on the front door. Yes, she's on the ground floor. And yes, it bothers me more than it should. I hear her voice getting louder the closer she gets to the door. Without missing a single note, she unlocks the door and opens it, letting me inside, all while belting out whatever garbage is playing on her phone.

She doesn't acknowledge me once I'm inside, too busy flitting around and doing whatever the hell it is girls do to "get ready". It allows me to look around her place without her jumping down my throat.

Freya's studio apartment is littered with the most random objects. A unicorn lamp sits on the bright red side table next to her bed, which is, of course, a complete mess. Her zebra sheets don't match the olive green and white polka dot comforter, both of which clash terribly with the assortment of throw pillows scattered about everywhere.

There's a string of chili pepper lights across the headboard and a rainbow-colored bead curtain pulled to one side, giving the illusion of privacy and separation from the rest of the room. Her place isn't messy, per se, but it's far from the minimalist style in my own home.

The thought of Freya's questionable décor, complete with frilly throw pillows, taking up space on my leather couch and gray bedspread flashes through my mind before I can stop it. In an attempt to distract myself from more unwelcome thoughts, I let my eyes wander to the woman I can't seem to get out of my head.

Freya has big, old-fashioned curlers in her bright red hair and some sort of white goop on her face. She's wearing a tight tank top that's stretched out over her ample chest and ratty yoga pants. The look is complete with fuzzy lime green flip-flop slippers. Her toes are painted a light blue to match the wedding colors.

I don't know why that detail in particular stands out. It's sweet. Not just the pastel color, but the fact that she wanted every feature to be perfect.

Something about seeing her like this, dancing around in her home wearing comfortable clothes, feels vulnerable. Like she's letting me in just a little bit. She could have yelled at me to stay out in the car while she finished up, and honestly, I expected her to. But here she is, seemingly comfortable having me hang around her space.

I wasn't sure what to expect after last night at the rehearsal dinner. I had been trying to ignore her in the green dress that hugged every single one of her curves when she suddenly excused herself from the table.

I don't know what happened exactly, but I could feel her distress when she finally sat back down. To her credit, she made a valiant effort to school her features, but there was no hiding the pale color that took over her face or the way her hand shook when she lifted her water glass. Something spooked Freya while she was gone, and that didn't sit right with me.

I tried convincing myself I was concerned because I didn't want anything to put a damper on the wedding festivities, but I know that's not true. Or at least it's not the whole truth. I was worried about her.

Gone was the lively woman who could spend hours teasing me and bringing me right to the edge of anger without actually pushing me over. In her place was a defensive and frightened little girl. I've never had the urge to take care of someone before, but fuck if I didn't want to know what was wrong so I could fix it.

Freya being Freya, however, snapped at me. If anyone else had spoken to me with such disdain and disrespect, I would have put them in their place. But Freya is different. I just didn't realize how different until last night.

The sound of a wailing cat pulls me back into the present. It's coming from the small bathroom next to the kitchen. At first, I think it's a new song Freya is trying to sing along to, but then she hollers out in pain. I'm across the small apartment in four strides, ripping the door open to get to her.

It takes me a few seconds to figure out what the hell is going on. Freya is flailing around the tiny bathroom, half cursing, half grunting, while fanning the side of her face. I notice the goop that was on her face is mostly washed off except for a patch over her forehead, right eye, and cheek.

She must have gotten some of the lotion or whatever the fuck in her eye. Without thinking about it, I cup her chin and turn her face towards me. To my shock, the frantic screeches and wild movements stop. Freya stands completely still, looking up at me with her one good eye.

I don't know why my skin isn't burning like it normally does when I touch someone, but I don't have time to dwell on that. Right now, I need to make sure Freya is okay and that she didn't cause permanent damage to her pretty eye.

I grab the nearest towel with my free hand and wet it down slightly before cleaning what's left of the gunk off of her face. I can't look at her piercing green eye, so I focus on gently wiping the cloth over her skin. When I get to her red, puffy, squinted eye, I use my thumb to gather up every last trace of the offending substance. Freya blinks a few times, and a tear forms and falls down her smooth, creamy cheek. I wipe that away, too.

Jesus, her skin is so damn soft. I can't remember the last time I had contact like this with another person. I wasn't lying when I told her no one touches me. What I didn't say is that it goes both ways. I don't like physical contact. I'm sure there's a connection somewhere between my ugly past and my aversion to touch, but I've never cared enough to connect the dots.

But feeling the heat of Freya's flushed skin triggers something inside of me. I want my hands all over her. I want to know if she's this silky smooth everywhere. I want to know if her blush stops at the swell of her tits or if it reaches all the way down to her blue-tipped painted toes.

I'm still holding her chin in one hand and gliding my thumb back and forth over her cheek with the other when Freya clears her throat and takes a step back. For the life of me, I can't understand the profound sense of loss now that my hands are not on her in some way.

"Thanks," she murmurs, trembling slightly. It appears that my touch affected her, too. In fact, I don't think I've seen her this still and quiet as long as I've known her. Is it really because of me? Did I somehow gain the ability to walk on water and calm the storm that is Freya Murphy?

"What was that shit anyway?" I grunt, taking another step back. I need to put some space between us, both physically and emotionally.

Freya sighs loudly, and I know she's finally snapped out of whatever spell we were both under. "I don't even know!" She whines, throwing her arms up and nearly knocking over a can of hairspray and a bag full of makeup. "It was a free sample of some face mask thing from work. It's supposed to make my skin radiant and energized, whatever the hell that means. How can skin be energized?"

I don't tell her that my skin is feeling energized, and it's not from wiping off the remnants of the face mask. My fingertips are still tingling with the memory of her warmth.

"Instead of radiant, I'm going to be the puffy-eyed girl who can't even put eyeliner on now!"

"You don't need makeup." Shit. Why did I say that? It's true, of course. Freya is undeniably gorgeous, even more so when she doesn't cover up her freckles or smear on eyeshadow that only serves to distract from her brilliant green eyes. But she doesn't need to know that. I suppose it's too late now.

Freya gives me a sassy little smile that does things to me. "You think I'm *preeeeetttttyyyyyyyy*!" She sing-songs. "I knew you liked me, Luca. I see right through your tough guy act. I have from day one, remember? All bark, no bite?"

Oh, but I want to bite you, baby girl.

Fuck. No. What? Shit.

"Ah-ha!" She exclaims. "No comeback for me? Not even a measly little grunt?"

I turn around and step out of the too-small bathroom, but not before growling at her for good measure. It just makes her laugh, and damn if that sound doesn't make me instantly hard. I just have to get through today. Then Freya will be out of my hair for a while.

That thought should bring me some relief, but instead, it makes my chest tight. I don't like it. Not one bit.

***

I can't take my eyes off Freya as she makes her way down the aisle with Darlene. I know the bride is supposed to be the most beautiful woman on her wedding day, but to me, Freya outshines everyone here. Hell, she outshines everyone in the city. I'm pretty sure she outshines everyone I've ever met. She's absolutely radiant, and it has nothing to do with the infamous face mask. It's all her.

The blue, gauzy dress she's wearing is fitted on top, clinging to the curve of her breasts and the slight dip in her waist. It flares out at her hips and drapes down in flowing layers all the way to the floor. I have to fight an honest to God smile when I see her light blue toes peeking out from the hem of the dress.

Freya lifts up Darlene's veil and smiles at her with all the love and joy in the world. Goddamn. I've never seen her smile so brightly. She has tears in her eyes, but they sparkle with complete happiness for her best friend. There's no doubt that Freya is as loyal as they come, once you break through her defenses, that is.

I can't see Matteo's face, but I'm sure he has that look of awe in his eyes, just like every time Darlene enters the room. I imagine his face looks similar to mine, only I'm staring at the complicated redhead who has gotten under my skin. And considering my aversion to touch, that's saying something.

Freya stares right back at me, those green eyes picking me apart and trying to figure out if I'm a threat to her. She's never been afraid of me, nor has she taken me seriously for a single second since I first talked to her over the phone. But right now, she's pretty damn serious. And she looks like she thinks I could destroy her. Doesn't she know she's the one with all the power here?

The priest clears his throat, and I swear I see Freya blush. It's not something she usually does, but I like the pink stain across her cheeks and down her neck. I wonder what else makes her blush. I wonder if she'll let me find out.

I shove those thoughts away, not able to process them just yet. I haven't been with anyone for nearly seventeen years. I was eighteen, and she was the only person I ever slept with. Turns out, having sex involves a lot of touching. And a lot of intimacy. I wasn't prepared for either of those things. But with Freya…

"Luca," Matteo whispers harshly. "The rings."

"Right," I say, shaking my head. Matteo gives me a knowing grin, which pisses me off. That seems to make him smile even more. I produce the rings from the inside pocket of my suit jacket and hand them over.

The priest recites the vows and Matteo and Darlene repeat them. The whole time, I can't stop looking at Freya. She can't seem to look away from me, either. I feel like I'm seeing her for the first time. No, that's not accurate. I feel like she's *letting* me see her for the first time.

Her normally sharp green eyes are softer. More vulnerable. She's every bit as stubborn and sassy as usual, and I already knew she was resilient and cunning, but I see more than that. There's a depth to her, a sadness, a longing so profound it nearly brings me to my knees.

The priest clears his throat again, which makes Freya blush and then look around her. I look around too, for the first time since she walked down the aisle. I notice that Darlene and Matteo are gone. How the hell did I miss their entire ceremony?

Freya takes a step towards me and grins. My stomach flips and an altogether unfamiliar feeling settles over me. I don't know what it means, but I think I like it.

"Psst," she whisper-shouts. "We're up."

I don't even try to contain the tiny smile that causes the corner of my mouth to curl up slightly. It's the same thing she said to me yesterday during the rehearsal, only this time, I'm not annoyed. What the hell changed in the last twenty-four hours?

Before I can fall further down that rabbit hole, Freya loops her arm in mine. This time, I don't protest. I only wish I wasn't wearing the button-up and suit jacket. I want to feel her soft skin rub against me. For the first time in my whole goddamn life, I want someone to touch me.

As if sensing the monumental shift deep in the core of who I am, Freya squeezes my arm a little tighter and leans into me. Fuck, it feels good. I have to actually fight the urge to sweep her up in my arms. I mean, what the hell?

Our arms stay linked as we walk through the library to another large room where the reception is being held. Freya is quiet the whole way there, which isn't like her at all. At first, I thought she was feeling all the confusing things I am, but that's not it.

The confident, playful woman who stepped off the stage with me falters a bit. It sounds cheesy as fuck, but I swear I can feel the energy around her change. Whatever she's feeling right now is weighing her down, dimming her light, and stealing her joy.

I don't get a chance to ask her what's wrong before she slips her arm out from underneath mine and goes off to talk to someone she must recognize. Not that I would know how to talk to her about emotional shit, but for the first time in my life, I want to try.

I get settled in at the table reserved for the wedding party, planning to stay planted right here, surveying the room for the remainder of the evening. I tell myself it's because I need to keep an eye on the guests and be ready to step in and ease any tension that could arise. A lot of people here were invited simply because of Matteo's position. It would be seen as a slight not to have esteemed members of organized crime in attendance.

But I know the real reason I'm scanning the room right now, and it has nothing to do with wanting to protect Matteo or the family. It's her. Of course, it's her. I can't let Freya out of my sight. Good thing her bright red hair makes it easy for me to keep an eye on her.

She smiles easily at everyone she greets, and she laughs with Darlene like she normally does, but I know it's not entirely genuine. I have the urge to go to her and demand she tell me what's wrong so I can fix it. The need to come to her rescue is just as strong as when I heard her distressed cries earlier today.

I watch her whisper something to Darlene and then slip out of the room. I know she's probably just going to the bathroom or something, but I don't like not having her in my line of vision. I wait a few moments before discreetly making my way towards the door Freya exited through.

As the underboss in one of the most revered crime families in Chicago, I've been in numerous situations that required stealth. My plan is to follow her from a distance. Just so I know she's okay. I'm sure Freya wouldn't appreciate having me tail her, but she won't see me. No harm, no foul, right?

When I step out into the hallway, I see Freya slumped against the wall with her arms wrapped around herself. She looks so damn small the way she's folded in on herself. I want to protect her from the world, even though I know she's strong enough to take on anyone and anything by herself. That's not the point. She shouldn't have to do it all alone.

"What the fuck are you doing here?" Freya hisses at me.

So much for going unnoticed. "How did you know I was following you?"

Instead of answering, Freya glares at me. She certainly has some secrets of her own. It's not the first time I've wondered about the way she grew up and how she seems to have "ninja skills" as Darlene puts it.

Darlene isn't wrong. Freya managed to put a tracking device in her best friend's necklace when they were just teens. She kept tabs on her best friend for years, which came in handy when Darlene was kidnapped a few months ago. Freya then managed to get my personal cell phone number so she could call and yell at me, and then she coordinated a plan of attack with the goddamn mafia to get Darlene back.

But right now, she looks every bit a twenty-one-year-old who is trying to find her way in the world. Jesus, it's easy to forget how damn young she is. Knowing she's fourteen years my junior should stop my growing obsession, I mean, *attraction* to her, but it only draws me closer.

"Look, Luca, I don't need a babysitter. I just needed some air," she huffs out.

I don't respond, I just lean against the wall at the end of the hallway, giving her plenty of space to work through whatever she needs to process.

"Seriously, you can leave now. I don't know if Leena sent you to check on me or whatever, but I'm fine."

I just nod and remain in place, watching over her. She looks irritated at my presence, but I can tell it's fake. She hasn't made a move to leave, after all.

"It's no big deal," Freya sighs. "I'm just all...I don't know. I'm feeling...things. It's the wedding, you know? It has my emotions all over the place. I'm happy for Leena. I really, truly am. She's the best person I know, and she deserves a happily ever after."

She pauses, trying to gather her thoughts. Freya didn't come right out and say it, but her words imply she doesn't deserve the same happily ever after her best friend got.

"Okay, fine. I'm going to miss her. Whatever. It's dumb. I mean, I know I can still see her, and she'll be my bestie and things aren't going to be all that different than they are now, but it *is* different. She's my...my person. But now she's Matteo's person, and Matteo is her person. Which is how it should be. I don't know shit about relationships, and even less about marriage, but I do know whoever your partner is should come first. I get it. But..." Freya sighs and shakes her head as she curls in on herself even more.

She didn't say it, but I know what she's thinking. She doesn't come first for Darlene anymore. She doesn't come first for anyone anymore, and that thought crushes her. I see it. I see her heart breaking.

Fuck, I feel like mine is cracking in two right along with her. I wish I knew how to put someone first. I want to be what she needs, but I've been a defective, fucked up asshole for as long as I can remember.

Music pours out into the hallway, making us both glance towards the door to the reception.

"There you two are!" Darlene says, looking between Freya and me with a not-so-subtle smile on her face. "Come on, it's time to cut the cake!"

I don't know how she does it, but Freya manages to dig up a genuine, heartfelt smile for her best friend as she skips towards her and grabs her hand. She looks completely recovered from her meltdown just moments ago. If I wasn't there to witness it myself, I'd never believe the woman chatting away happily with Darlene had any insecurities or worries at all.

The two women walk ahead of me, going on and on about the decor and the food and the live band. I, on the other hand, can't stop picturing Freya in my arms. In my bed. In my life as more than just Matteo's wife's annoying best friend. I can't help but imagine a future with the disaster of a woman with secrets, complications, and a vulnerable side that runs deeper than I could have ever imagined.

Chapter 4

Freya

My alarm went off an hour ago, but I can't seem to bring myself to get out of bed. I woke up with an ache in my chest. At first, I thought it was because Darlene is officially a married woman which means she's Matteo's best friend now, and not mine. I know that's a shitty way to look at it, but that's where I'm at right now.

The longer I'm wrapped up in my blankets and my despairing thoughts, the more I realize it's not about Darlene at all. Well, okay, maybe a little bit. But the tightness in my chest is from Luca. My heart squeezes and thuds around in my ribcage when I think about his touch. It was brief but surprisingly gentle. He cleaned me up and wiped away my tears and then just...held my face in his hands. It made me feel things I've never even thought. I felt precious. Fragile, but safe.

I felt the same way when he followed me out into the hallway and just stood there during the reception. Luca hardly spoke more than five words to me, and yet he managed to get me to spill my guts. What is it about this man that gets me all worked up?

Obviously, he's sexy as fuck. I've always thought so. I'm sure I'm not alone in my astute observation. And I've always enjoyed trying to get a reaction out of him, because how could I not? The perpetually perturbed beast is endearing in his own way.

But last night was different. We connected in a way that made me feel incredibly vulnerable, but not weak. I put myself at his mercy by telling him all my private thoughts and stupid insecurities, but he didn't take advantage of my trust. He let me wrestle with everything without swooping in to save the day, which I appreciated.

And what the hell was going on during the ceremony? I barely remember anything the priest said. I don't think I even noticed when he pronounced Matteo and Darlene husband and wife. I was too busy being hypnotized by Luca's intense, deep blue eyes.

"Goddamnit!" I shout to the universe. Or, rather, to my upstairs neighbor who stomps on his floor to let me know I'm being too loud. He does this quite often.

Unwilling to untangle whatever knot of emotions I now have towards Luca; I roll out of bed and grab my laptop. Work always provides a good distraction. No, it's not a new job. In fact, it's a very old job. My first job, actually.

I'm a hacker.

I learned how to track people down and steal from them thanks to dear ol' dad, though I was always better at it than he was. I had to be. My dad got himself into some fucked up situations and I was his secret weapon. Until he sold me out.

I'm not rich by any means, but I do okay for myself. I could definitely afford a better apartment, but this one is small and unassuming, which suits me just fine.

The life of a hacker isn't all covert missions and stealing government secrets. At least it isn't for me. I only take small jobs that won't make much of a difference in the world except for the person paying for my services. Honestly, I'm more of a private investigator with a focus on digital tracking and online accounts.

Some jobs are basically Facebook stalking someone for an older client who doesn't understand social media. It's easy money and I don't feel bad about charging an arm and a leg to do it. It's the client's fault for being naïve enough to hand over money for something they could figure out themselves. Other jobs are more complex, like gathering information on important CEOs or getting private tax information and bank account logins.

My biggest accomplishment to date, however, was getting Luca's phone number. It required some acting on my part, which is never a part of any other job I take on, but this one was obviously a special case. I managed to track down his phone carrier and then called the store, pretending to be Luca's assistant.

With the amount of information I already had on Luca, Matteo, and few other key players in the Moscatelli crime family, it was surprisingly easy to answer all the questions about the account designed for the purpose of keeping hackers like me away.

After passing the first hurdle, all it took was a fake story about my new, high-maintenance boss demanding that I change his number since he was far too important to bother himself with such menial tasks. The lady on the other end of the line took the bait, and we started swapping stories about our bosses. I got her so distracted, she didn't ask me to confirm the old number before cutting service and switching over to the new phone number. Sucker.

I boot up my computer and check a few emails via the encrypted server I have set up for client-hacker purposes only, dismissing most of the cases without responding. I'm very picky about the clients and jobs I take on.

My phone rings, pulling me from my trance of emails and research. It's Heather from my current part-time job and Bath Bombs Galore & More. Yeah, I definitely need to quit. I obviously don't need the money, but I have to keep up appearances. Plus, I wasn't lying when I told Luca I like bouncing around from job to job. Without the pressure of needing to earn a paycheck, I mostly enjoy all the side gigs and new experiences.

"Hey, Heather," I sigh, already not looking forward to this conversation.

"Freya," she clips out. "I wasn't going to call you on your day off, but I'm afraid I didn't have a choice. I don't want you coming in tomorrow. Or ever again."

I swallow down a laugh at the uptight, middle-aged store manager who wears blue eyeshadow and Crocs to work. She's trying to be threatening, but it comes across as whiney.

"Oh?" I ask innocently. I know exactly what's going on and why she fired me without actually telling me I'm fired, but I want her to squirm a little bit. I can't help it. She's a total bitch who thinks she's better than her employees.

"Well, yes. I assume you are aware yelling at customers is unacceptable."

"Hmm. Yelling at customers doesn't sound like me," I say sweetly.

"Are you kidding me?" She mutters. "Anyway, it doesn't matter. You are relieved of your duties as an employee at BBG and M."

I snort at her abbreviation for the store. She's the only one who calls it that, and she sounds ridiculous every time she does it. The way she makes it sound like being employed at *BBG and M* is equivalent to serving in the military pushes me over the edge. I start laughing into the phone, spurred on by her indignant gasp.

"No worries Heather. Thanks for the laugh!" I hang up before she has a chance to respond. That's one thing off my to-do list. Maybe today won't be so bad after all.

A movement right outside the window catches my eye. I duck down out of habit, hiding behind the small dining room table. The curtain is closed, but it's a sheer material, so I can still make out basic shapes. I don't see anything at first, but the overgrown bush to the side of my window shakes. I hear the leaves rustle and the small branches scrape against the glass.

Someone is out there. Someone is watching me. The same fear and sense of dread that I felt at the rehearsal dinner floods my system. I thought someone was watching me then, too, but I convinced myself it was nothing.

This isn't nothing.

I crawl on my hands and knees through the kitchen and into the small bathroom. I get in the shower and pull the curtain closed before sitting on the floor and making myself as small as possible. I clutch my phone as if it's some lifeline, and without thinking, I navigate over to Luca's number. The one he never bothered to change back. It makes me smile every time I think about it.

My thumb hovers over the call button. I might annoy and confuse him, but I think he'd help me if I called him. He'd do it for Darlene and Matteo, if nothing else. That thought both comforts me and makes me bristle. I don't need anyone to save me, especially not a man.

After a few minutes of not hearing anything, I slowly stand up and take a few tentative steps towards the bathroom door. Taking a deep, calming breath, I walk out into my kitchen, making a beeline towards my purse where I keep my gun. It's just a tiny thing, but a bullet's a bullet, right?

I sit cross-legged on my bed, holding my gun at the ready just in case someone bursts through the window or the front door. I don't know how much time has passed, but my legs are numb from the way I've been sitting, and my muscles ache from tensing for so long.

What did I really see, anyway? Just a shadow and a bush moving. It could have been my neighbor walking outside and then a rabbit hiding in the bushes or something. No need to draw a gun, for Christ's sake. I'm losing it. I blame Luca. It's his fault I woke up in a weird mood.

I shake my head at my ridiculous self and put the gun away. I need to get some fresh air and leave my apartment full of weird, confusing thoughts. Maybe I could visit the animal shelter I used to work at. Petting puppies and little furry kittens sounds pretty great right about now. At the very least, it will provide a distraction from whatever the hell is going on in my head.

Chapter 5

Luca

I hear her before I see her, which is often the case with Freya. Darlene and Matteo left early this morning for their week-long honeymoon, which means Freya is here to see me. There's a queasy feeling in my stomach. Wait, no. It's not that. It's...excitement? Nerves? It's altogether unfamiliar, which is something I'm starting to get used to whenever Freya is around. That woman has me thinking and feeling things I don't even know how to name, let alone decipher.

The door to my office swings open and bangs against the wall. The chaotic woman I've been obsessing over ever since I left the wedding last night appears in the doorway, looking wild and frantic.

I immediately stand up and feel the need to give her a hug, which is another new thing for me. I want to fix whatever has her looking so wide-eyed and panicky.

"Freya, what's—"

My question is cut off by a whine and a bark. It's then I notice the giant bag Freya has clutched to her side. It's moving. And barking. Freya kicks the door closed and then carefully sets the bag on the ground. More yips and barks fill the room as she scoops out not one, but two little dogs. Then she reaches back into the bag and cradles a tiny kitten in her hands.

This is certainly not how I thought my morning would go.

"Explain," I demand.

"Okay, so hear me out. I went to the animal shelter I used to work at because I needed to get out of my apartment with the weird vibes and creepy bush and so I thought, 'puppies make everything better', and then I got there and found out two of my favorite little furballs were going to be sent to a kill shelter at the end of the week, and since I'm a decent human being and not a fucking monster, I obviously had to do something about it. I may have sort of stolen them. I mean *rescued* them. I saved their lives! I'm a hero! But unfortunately, I'm a hero who lives in a studio apartment and I can't have pets and also I think the animal shelter people are probably looking for me because I wasn't exactly subtle in my departure."

I stare at Freya while she catches her breath from her rambling explanation. This woman. She's good at getting herself into trouble. Not so much at getting herself out of it. I should be annoyed. Frustrated. Angry. But instead, I'm fighting off a goddamn smile at the thought of Freya trying to subtly do anything, let alone break animals out of an animal shelter.

One of the dogs barks and nips playfully at Freya's shoelace.

"You were no help at all, mister," she scolds, though her face is soft and full of love. "You couldn't keep quiet for ten minutes, could you?" The dog barks and wags its tail, excited at the attention it's getting. Freya sets the cat down gently on the floor and scratches behind the little mutt's ears.

I ignore how cute it is, as well as the fact that I just thought the word *cute*, and try to parse out what she just told me.

"Why do you have three animals if only two were going to the kill shelter?" It's probably not the most important question that needs to be addressed, but I find I want to know how her mind works and what her motivations are. I want to know every single thing about her. The craziest fucking thing of all is that I want her to know about me, too.

"They are brothers! How could I possibly separate them?!" Freya looks horrified that I would even suggest such a thing.

"They are...brothers? You know one's a cat, right?" I don't bother pointing out the fact that one dog has long, wiry, brown fur, while the other has short, white fur with brown spots. Clearly, none of them are actually related. Then again, neither are her and Darlene, yet they're closer than any family I've ever known or seen.

She narrows her eyes at me and scowls. I bite back a groan as my cock twitches to life, making my pants uncomfortably tight. I sit back down, hoping to hide my growing issue behind the safety of my desk.

Freya covers the cat's ears and whispers, "He has a complex, okay? I told him he could be whoever he wants, and I'd love him all the same. Doesn't everyone deserve that?"

Well, that just about fucking guts me. Freya is brilliant and strong and guarded, but she has these moments of raw vulnerability. Whether she knows it or not, she's talking about herself more than her confused feline friend.

I run my hand through my hair and take a deep breath. I'm totally out of my element here. Animals, a fiery, mesmerizing woman, lust, empathy, possessiveness. This is uncharted territory and I don't want to fuck it up, whatever "it" is. Her heart? My heart? Shit.

"What do you want me to do with this information?" I ask slowly, not wanting to set her off again.

I know I'm in trouble when Freya flashes me a heart-stopping smile. It's too sweet, a little manipulative, but beautiful all the same. I have no idea what she's about to ask me to do, but I'm pretty sure I'm going to do it. Today just keeps throwing me curveballs.

"Well...I was hoping you could like, pull some mafia strings and get the shelter to back off? I can't say for sure they called the cops, but Joni, the manager, didn't take too kindly to me liberating three pups."

The corners of my lips curl up into a small little smirk, but I hide it as quickly as it appears. Only Freya could break the law and sound completely indignant that anyone would try to stop her.

"Mafia strings?" I question, trying to keep a stern look on my face, but failing miserably.

"Yeah, I mean, there have to be some benefits to the whole organized crime family thing, right? I'm not saying you should rough Joni up or anything. Don't break her kneecaps, okay? Just, like, I don't know. Imply that things might not go well for her if she pursues legal action against me."

"Let me get this straight. You want me to threaten the manager of an animal shelter?"

"It was just a suggestion. I don't want to tell you how to do your job. You do whatever you think fits the situation," she says in all seriousness as if she's being generous and accommodating.

"I've never been in a situation like this before," I grumble, wiping a hand down my face. This woman. She's too much. No, that's not accurate. She's perfect, and that scares the shit out of me. I get that feeling again. The one that tells me I can't fuck this up. "Okay," I say finally.

"Okay?"

I nod, starting to form an idea of how to get her out of this mess. Obviously, I'm not going to threaten an animal shelter employee. That's just overkill. But I can have the animals officially adopted and strongly suggest the shelter forget about the little jailbreak. A sizable donation should do the trick.

"Okay!" Freya claps her hands. The little spark of joy and relief in her eyes makes it worth all the hassle and headache.

She picks up the cat and sits on the couch, settling the furry creature in her lap before helping the little dogs onto the couch. Their stubby legs make it difficult for them to jump that high. I should be annoyed that the mutts are shedding all over the five thousand dollar, Italian leather couch, but when the animals curl up on either side of Freya and lay their heads in her lap, I feel nothing but warmth. It's strange, but I'm starting to get used to it. Much like everything Freya makes me feel.

We sit in silence for a few moments. Freya takes turns scratching behind each dog's ears and rubbing their bellies and then cooing over the kitten sleeping soundly in her lap.

I want her to pet me that way.

The thought hits me right in the chest. I'm jealous of a damn dog. Not only that, but I crave her touch. I can almost feel her soft fingers stroking up and down my face. My chest. My cock.

Get it the fuck together.

"There's one more thing," Freya breaks the silence. She plasters on her best innocent face, but she's not fooling me. I like seeing her try, though. It's...cute.

I tip my head and gesture with my hand for her to continue.

"Remember the part about me living in a studio apartment and not being able to have pets?"

"Oh, no, no, no. You're not suggesting that I – "

"You'll absolutely *adore* Larry, Curly, and Mo." I stare at her, waiting for her to tell me those names are a joke. She doesn't. "You know. Like the Three Stooges?" Freya clarifies as if I don't get the reference.

Instead of rolling my eyes, I find myself asking who's who. This makes Freya smile so big I feel it deep in my chest.

"This one over here is Curly," she informs me, petting the dog on her right. "Because of his brown fuzzy curls, of course. And this little bundle of floofins is Mo, obviously," Freya says, petting the cat.

"Obviously," I mumble. Freya glares at me but then grins. My cock surges to life once again.

"Which just leaves little Larry here."

"And what exactly am I supposed to do with them?"

Freya's laugh echoes around the room and rattles through my body. It's a rich, hearty sound that fills me up and makes me forget everything except her.

"Take care of them!"

"How?"

"Just love them, you know?"

"How?" I ask again, though I didn't mean to say it out loud.

She gives me a soft smile, one I've never seen before. "There's the basics, of course. Food, water, playtime. Beyond that, just get to know them. They'll show you what they need, all you have to do is pay attention."

"You make it sound so easy."

Freya shrugs. "With animals, it is."

"Just animals, huh?"

She shrugs again, breaking eye contact with me so she can play with Curly's long fur. "Humans are more...complicated. I don't really know anything about loving anyone. Darlene is the only one who puts up with me, and she's pretty easy to love."

God, this woman. I wasn't sure if she felt whatever I did yesterday at the wedding, but now I know she did. She had to have felt the connection we shared if she's willing to be this open with me.

Freya leans down and whispers something into Larry's ear, then sets him down on the floor and pats his wiggling butt to encourage him to move. I watch the fuzzy mutt walk towards me, wagging his tail so hard the entire back half of his body moves with it.

Larry sits in front of me and yips expectantly. What the hell do I do with him? We stare at each other, both seemingly waiting for the other one to make the first move. He scoots his butt closer to me, his tail still working overtime, thudding against the floor.

He whines and gives me the most pathetic look. Part of me doesn't want to reward his behavior, nor Freya's, for that matter. But the bigger part of me already knows I'm going to give in to her request. How could I not? She looked so content with those animals all curled up around her.

I think back to yesterday when she confessed to missing Darlene. Freya deserves some loyal friends. Plus, if I keep the pets, she'll have to come and visit them. It's that thought that sends me over the edge.

I tentatively reach my hand out, not sure if the little guy wants to sniff me, lick me, or bite me. I'm at his mercy just as much as I am Freya's. Larry sniffs my hand and then flops on his back, showing me his belly.

Freya laughs softly, making me look over at her. She nods, encouraging me to pet the little monster. So, I do. I rub his belly and watch him stretch and wiggle and sigh contentedly. Soon, Larry is joined by Curly, who is apparently jealous. I give him the same attention. Mo meanders over, stepping right over his brothers and nuzzling my hand.

I don't even try to stop the smile that takes over my face. Who knew animals were so great?

Freya joins my new companions, kneeling down on the floor next to them and giving them attention and love, which all three eat up greedily. She looks up at me and gives me that same soft smile, though this time I swear I see tears shining in her clear green eyes.

"Thank you," she murmurs. She's thanking me for so much more than taking in these stray pets, but we don't need to talk about it. It's enough that we both know.

I clear my throat and sit up in my chair. "What now?"

"Now we go to the pet store, obviously," Freya says, grinning playfully.

"I can send someone to get whatever they need."

"Where's the fun in that? Don't you want to pick out the toys yourself? They probably need collars, too. If you send some rando to the store who hasn't even met the Three Stooges, how will he know what to get?" Freya explains all of this as if it were the most reasonable thing in the world.

Do I want to spend the day selecting dog toys and discussing the pros and cons of pet food? Not even a little bit. Nevertheless, I find myself agreeing to whatever she wants.

Chapter 6

Freya

Luca is standing in the middle of Pet Paradise with a cart full of squeaky toys, water bowls, rawhides, catnip mice, and three big, fluffy beds that will probably never be used. I have to bite my lips to hide my smile. This gigantic man in a three-piece suit looks completely out of place, which only makes me like him more.

I don't know how I ended up in Luca's office, begging him to bail me out and take Larry, Curly, and Mo. One minute I was driving like a bat out of hell with the Three Stooges in tow, and the next minute I was running through the compound to find Luca. I somehow just knew he'd fix everything.

Something is different between us today. Could the mountain of a man with a fortress around his heart almost as impenetrable as mine be feeling the same confusing things I am? I saw something in his striking blue eyes when I thanked him. I felt safe. How crazy is that?

I shake my head of those thoughts, focusing instead on the important task of selecting collars.

"Do you think Mo would like pink rhinestones or purple rhinestones on his collar?" I turn to look at Luca, who is trying his best to be grumpy. It only makes him look pouty, like an adorable toddler determined not to have a good time.

"I think since he's a boy, pink and purple rhinestones aren't appropriate," he grunts.

"First of all, get that toxic masculinity bullshit out of here. Rhinestones are fabulous regardless of gender, and the idea of pink and purple being feminine colors is simply a product of our society."

Luca could not look more shocked if an elephant dressed in a bikini stampeded through the store. I like this look on him. He opens his mouth and then closes it again. Have I made the big, scary, mafia man squirm? Today just keeps getting better and better.

"And second of all, you're right. Mo wouldn't like rhinestones. I was just testing you to see if you guys connected the way I thought you did." Luca narrows his eyes at me, but I see him fighting a smile. I wish he would show me his real smile. I wonder when was the last time he used it. "What do you think Mo would like?"

I expect him to roll his eyes at me and scoff, but to my surprise, Luca turns to face the wall of cat collars. His brow furrows in concentration, and I can't help the cheesy grin that spreads across my face. He's taking it so *seriously*, much like he does everything in life.

After studying the choices for a few moments, Luca tentatively reaches out for a blue camo collar, but then hesitates and moves over to a royal blue collar with white polka dots on it. His fingers hover in front of the collar, then Luca looks over at me with an eyebrow raised, as if asking my permission. Fuck, I'm enjoying this too much. I'm enjoying *him* too much.

I nod and smile, letting him know I'm pleased with his choice. Luca exhales like he was holding his breath until he knew I approved. I won't lie, knowing I have some control over him makes me feel powerful in a way I've never experienced. Luca is not the man I thought he was. He's kind of...perfect.

My chest gets that achy feeling I had this morning. I don't know what it means, just that he's the only person who has ever made me feel this way. And it's not just my heart that's aching; my lady parts have been throbbing ever since I burst into his office and saw him sitting behind his solid oak desk, every bit the sexy, formidable man of my dirty fantasies.

"You okay?" Luca asks, his deep voice startling me out of my thoughts once more.

"Y-yeah. What's up?"

Luca's eyes twinkle, and yeah, it makes my pussy clench up and release an embarrassing amount of wetness.

"You just looked flushed is all. Are you hot, Freya?"

Good God, is that a smirk on his face? Is Luca flirting with me?

"I, um, right, a little warm," I stammer out like an idiot. I may be tough as shit, but I know nothing about men or flirting or relationships. Not that we'd ever be in a relationship or whatever. I'm just saying.

I clear my throat and clap my hands together in an attempt to get things back on track. "I think we've done enough damage for today," I say, surveying the cart full of goodies. Luca nods and follows me up to the register.

I briefly consider paying for all of the pet stuff, seeing as I rescued the Three Stooges and thrust them upon Luca, but then I remember he has access to piles of money. Luca raises an eyebrow at me, a tiny little grin tugging at his lips as if he knew exactly what I was thinking.

"Don't worry, I'll let you get it," I smile sweetly at him and bat my eyelashes dramatically, hoping to get him to grin a little more. The man is always sexy, but the little glimpses of his smile make him absolutely devastating.

Luca walks beside me, dutifully pushing the cart through the parking lot. The moment is so...domestic. Like we're a normal couple running errands on a Saturday afternoon. I never thought I wanted that life, but I don't think I'd mind if Luca was by my side. Not that we'd ever have a "normal" life considering his profession, but still. It feels like a major revelation.

A blur of black catches my eye. I swear someone just ducked behind a car across the aisle. My heart stops in my chest and I freeze in place. Luca pushes me behind him, and I follow his silent command, fisting the back of his jacket until my knuckles turn white.

"What is it? What's wrong?" He asks. His tone is soft, so as not to be heard, but laced with a dangerous threat. Luca has a tight grip on my hip, holding me in place, and I see his other hand reach for his gun. Something about that makes me come to my senses. I loosen my hold on his jacket, smoothing out the wrinkles.

"It's okay, I'm okay. I just had a scare," I whisper.

Luca grunts in acknowledgment but doesn't let go of me or the gun. I take a deep breath, feeling embarrassed both at my paranoia and my reaction. I've never let someone jump in and take care of me. Then again, no one has ever offered.

Luca's reaction was automatic. He had no idea what the perceived threat was, but he put himself in between me and danger. The man was, and still is, ready to take a bullet for me. It's that thought that finally gives me the strength to move out from behind him.

"Hey," I say gently, taking in his tense facial features, his protective stance, and the way his muscles are wound tight, ready for an attack. Luca glances down at me, his sharp blue eyes roaming up and down my face, checking for distress. "I overreacted. It was nothing."

When he still doesn't take his hand off the gun tucked into the waistband of his pants, I reach out and brush my fingers over his. Luca looks at our hands, then flicks his eyes back to mine. I can see the tension in his body easing ever so much, though he still looks hyperaware of our surroundings.

He nods his head once, then releases his grip on the gun. Before I even have time to register what's happening, Luca flips his hand over and laces our fingers together. He tugs me along and deposits me in the passenger seat of his car. Luca silently leans in and fastens my seatbelt for me, not letting go of my hand until he absolutely has to.

If anyone else on the planet buckled me into a car, I would claw their eyes out and let them know exactly what I think about their controlling, possessive behavior. But when Luca does it, I feel safe. Precious, even. It's probably just the adrenaline, though. At least that's the story I'm telling myself.

The drive to Luca's place is filled with a heavy silence. I can feel the tension rippling off him. I know he has questions, but I pray he doesn't ask them. I'm not ready to answer. I'm not ready to lose him.

We pull into the driveway of his enormous house, just a few minutes from the Moscatelli compound. I'm grateful for the distraction of unloading all the pet supplies. I feel so stupid for ruining our outing. We were having fun, and I even got Luca to almost smile, but then I messed it all up by freaking the fuck out for no reason.

Luca unlocks the door, and I'm greeted by two excited, wiggly puppies and one cat - er, dog, pretending to be aloof, yet making his way over to me all the same. I drop the bags on the floor and kneel in front of the little floof balls, soaking up all the love they are willing to give.

When Curly starts rooting around in one of the bags on the floor, I laugh and open up the package of rawhide bones, handing one each to Curly and Larry. Mo looks at me expectantly, so I hand him one too. It's far too big, but the little guy drags it across the floor and joins his brothers, who are happily chewing on their new toys over by the fireplace.

I feel exposed now that I don't have the buffer of the Three Stooges. What must Luca think of me? He hasn't said a single thing since leaving the store. I wouldn't blame him if he sent me on my way. I've caused plenty of trouble for one day.

I tilt my head up and see Luca standing in front of me, giving me a look I've never seen before. It's part confusion, part concern, and part...I don't know. Something else. Something deeper. Something terrifying and exhilarating and overwhelming.

He continues to stare at me as I stand up, then Luca takes a step forward, crowding my space. I instinctively take a step back, but Luca follows my movement until my back is pressed against the wall.

Luca is so close to me, I can feel his breath on my lips and the heat of his body, mere inches from mine. Out of the corner of my eye, I see his hand moving up towards my face, but then he falters and drops it by his side again. I've never seen Luca unsure of anything, but right now, he seems vulnerable. Almost fragile, though I know that can't be right.

"I have to try something," he murmurs so quietly I barely hear him. I nod, not knowing what I'm agreeing to, but absolutely sure I'd do anything for this man right now.

Luca raises his hand again, more steadily this time with my permission. Knowing the dominating, powerful underboss of the Moscatelli crime family wants my consent before touching me settles something deep inside.

He ghosts his fingers over my temple and down my cheek, in the softest whisper of a touch. A shiver runs down my spine, making me clench my thighs together. Luca trails his fingertips down my neck, pausing to draw circles over my pounding pulse point. My breath catches in my throat and I tilt my head to the side, giving him better access.

Luca growls softly and continues his featherlight touches across my skin. He's studying every single inch he touches as if it's some great mystery to him. I'm a trembling mess by the time his eyes meet mine again. He holds my gaze for a second, and then slowly leans in, brushing his lips across my temple, breathing me in and then following the same path his fingers took.

When he gets to my pulse point, Luca presses a soft kiss over the sensitive spot, making me gasp. He makes a noise in the back of his throat as if he's confirming something. Then I feel his hot, wet tongue slide across my skin, pushing against my throbbing pulse.

A moan escapes my lips, which causes Luca to grunt and scrape his teeth over the same spot. My entire body is desperate for him, aching to be touched for real, to be kissed, to be...his.

As if sensing my thoughts, Luca lifts his head and cups my face in his large, capable hands, forcing me to hold his fierce gaze. His parted lips hover above mine, making my heart pound wildly. I can feel each erratic beat in my clit, each pulse sending shockwaves throughout my body. An excruciating need I've never felt before courses through my veins, stealing my breath and making my bones vibrate.

Luca rests his forehead against mine and presses his body into me, pinning me against the wall with his large frame. I'm completely surrounded by his muscles, his scent, his bright blue eyes, shining with lust and longing.

I lick my suddenly dry lips, making Luca's jaw clench. His muscles flex against my soft curves, and then I feel his hardness grind against my stomach. I feel overwhelming heat and pressure building up in my core and spreading outward with each breath we draw together. I whimper, but the sound is cut short when his mouth crashes down over mine.

Luca's hands tangle in my hair and pull me closer. He licks the seam of my lips and thrusts his tongue inside my mouth.

I cry out in shock as an unexpected orgasm rips through me. My body is engulfed in white-hot flames of pleasure. I gasp for air, not understanding my body's reaction to this man. Luca growls and blazes a trail of kisses down my neck as he slides his hands down my body and grips the back of my thighs.

My orgasm continues to devastate me as he lifts me up and wraps my legs around his hips. I grip his shoulders and kiss this intoxicating man again as he grinds his hard cock into my soaking wet core.

Each time Luca's thickness rubs against my clit, my pussy spasms, begging to be filled. He grunts and rolls his hips, sucking on my neck, my collarbone, my heaving chest. My limbs are trembling and my head spins as I dig my fingernails into the nape of his neck. Luca lifts his head and captures my lips once again in a searing kiss.

We're both panting for air by the time he tears his mouth from mine. He rests his cheek against mine as we both try to catch our breath.

"What are you doing to me?" He whispers. I feel his lips move against the shell of my ear as he forms each word. I don't think he meant to say it out loud, but I'm glad he did. I'm glad I'm not the only one feeling this. Whatever "this" is.

Luca slides me down his body and sets me on the ground. My knees wobble a bit, but he keeps a tight grip on my hips, steadying me until I can stand on my own. He steps away from me, and a biting chill sweeps through my body. I don't like not having him near me. God, who am I right now?

I brush my fingers over my swollen lips, still unable to wrap my head around what just happened. Luca shoves a hand through his hair and then rubs the back of his neck like he's not sure where to go from here. I don't know either, but I know we'll never go back to the way things were before.

Chapter 7

Luca

I dropped Freya off yesterday afternoon after the kiss that completely ruined me. I don't know what I was thinking, but I don't regret it.

Something snapped inside me when she froze in the parking lot. I could smell the fear rolling off of her in waves. I didn't have time to think about it, I just shoved her behind me and prepared to kill any motherfucker who made her feel this way.

Even when Freya told me she was fine, I couldn't seem to relax until her delicate little hand rested on top of mine. I don't know what the fuck made her afraid, but I know she'll tell me when she's ready. There's so much more to Freya than meets the eye, and I find myself wanting to know all of her secrets.

In my line of work, information is the most powerful weapon. It can keep us out of trouble with the authorities, be used as blackmail, and help us understand our enemy's weaknesses so we can defeat them.

But I don't want to know Freya's secrets so I can manipulate or dominate her. I want to protect those fragile parts she holds so closely. I want to share her pain and cover her weaknesses instead of exploit them.

As if that wasn't enough of a paradigm shifting revelation, I was drawn to her creamy skin and vulnerable green eyes. I felt her, kissed her, fucking mauled the poor girl in my desperate need to be closer, have more, meld our goddamn souls together. She didn't protest, though. In fact, my kiss somehow brought her to a trembling orgasm. I felt like the most powerful man in the whole fucking world.

But then it became too much. She felt too good, tasted too good, hell, she's just too damn good for me in general. Her touch unraveled me and I panicked, not knowing if I'd ever be able to pull myself together again. I'm still wrecked, and it's been nearly thirty-six hours since I dropped her off. Not that I'm counting or anything.

Who am I kidding? I couldn't stop thinking about her all day today. I was distracted and more short-tempered than usual, which is saying something. I roll my eyes just thinking about my ludicrous behavior as if I'm some teenager with a silly crush. I finally understand why Matteo was so absentminded while he and Darlene were working things out. It annoyed me to no end, but now I get it.

"Fuck," I mutter to myself, rolling over in my bed and trying to find a comfortable position. I've been lying here, awake for hours, trying to come to terms with the fact that my bed feels empty, despite Larry, Curly, and Mo taking up the entire right side. My body craves Freya's, but my mind is throwing out warning signals. And my heart? I can't say that I've ever considered it worthy of weighing in on any decision I've ever made.

My phone rings, the loud sound piercing through my thoughts. I groan and wipe my hands down my face, trying to recalibrate after my confusing as fuck evening. It's nearly one in the morning, but I'm always on call. Even more so since Matteo is on his honeymoon.

60

I reach for the offending phone and freeze when I see Freya's name flash across the screen. My usually aloof and gruff attitude shatters at the thought of her being in danger.

"What's wrong?" I grunt into the phone as I hop out of bed and scramble to find clothes so I can get to her place as soon as possible.

I hear her take a shaky breath and blow it out. Every single muscle in my body tightens and coils, ready to spring into action.

"I-I... I think someone is outside," she whispers.

Overwhelming anger and fear wash over me. I'm not a man who scares easily, or at all, really, but I can admit that I'm freaking the fuck out knowing I'm a good fifteen minutes away from her.

"Go sit in your shower with the curtain drawn. I'll be there soon." My voice is harsher than I meant it to be, but fuck, I can't be blamed. This isn't the time for niceties, it's the time for action.

"No, no, I'm sorry. It's probably the storm. I don't know why I even called. It just sort of happened and now we're talking, but I'm being paranoid. It's the storm. I'm sure it's just the storm," Freya repeats, though I think she's trying to convince herself more than me.

"Storm?" I ask, putting my phone on speaker so I can throw on a shirt and hop into a pair of jeans.

"Yeah, can't you hear it?"

I pause to listen for a storm. Sure enough, the wind is howling, and rain pelts the windows of my house. I was so consumed with my thoughts about Freya I didn't even hear a fucking thunderstorm.

"I'm coming over."

"Wait, no, that's really not necessary, I have a gun, and—"

"End of discussion," I growl. It doesn't surprise me in the least that Freya is packing heat, but the thought of her being in a position to use it makes me see red. "Keep your phone on you and call me if you hear anything else."

"Excuse me? End of discussion? Who the hell do you think you—"

"I'll be there in fifteen minutes. No, seven." Fuck the speed limit. My Audi R8 tops out at two-hundred miles per hour. I won't be driving it quite that fast, but it's good to know I have that option in case Freya calls again before I get there.

I hang up before she can protest even more.

Six and a half minutes later, I pull into the parking lot of Freya's building, haphazardly parking my one hundred and seventy five thousand dollar car half in the handicapped spot and half on the sidewalk leading up to her apartment.

I hold my gun at my side, ready to take out anyone lingering around Freya's windows or front door. I fucking hate that she has a first-floor apartment. That shit is going to have to change. I can't be losing sleep knowing she's at risk.

When I reach her apartment, I rap my knuckles on her door and call out her name. Seconds later, it swings open, revealing a disheveled Freya with wild hair, a ratty old t-shirt, and terry cloth pajama shorts that I already know are going to be a distraction.

"Luca, I told you not to—"

I cut her off by resting my hands on her shoulders and walking her backward inside her apartment. I follow her, locking the door behind me and quickly scanning the small space, looking for any threats. Satisfied when I don't find anything, I click the safety on my gun and tuck it into the waistband of my jeans.

"Pack your shit, let's go," I command, looking over my shoulder and glancing out the window. "Hurry up," I bark. "I'll keep watch while you get what you need."

When I don't hear her moving, I reluctantly turn to face her. I'm greeted with one pissed off Freya, complete with her hands on her hips and a scowl on her face. "I'm not going with you."

I stare at her, trying to figure out what she wants from me. "Fine, I'll stay here then. Do you have an extra pillow and blanket?" I grumble, not happy about the prospect of sleeping on the floor in clothes wet from the rain. Plus, the Three Stooges are probably wondering where I am. I scoff at myself for becoming such a pussy in the last few days.

"No, I don't, but it doesn't matter, because you're not staying here."

I ball my fists up at my sides, staring at the gorgeous, infuriating woman in front of me. "Then why am I here?" I grit out through clenched teeth.

"I told you not to come!" Freya says exasperatedly, throwing her hands up and then pacing around her small studio apartment.

My frustration and worry boil over into anger. "What kind of game is this? Do you enjoy fucking with me?"

"Not this time. Not about this," she says firmly, narrowing her eyes in my direction. "I already told you I don't know why I called. I didn't ask you to come over, or for you to stay, or for you to take me to your place."

"Well, what the hell did you think I was going to do? You call crying in the middle of the goddamn night telling me some fucker is outside your place, of course, I'm going to come over," I practically yell.

"I didn't cry!" She stomps her foot indignantly. Her eyes let me know she's trying with all her might to summon a lightning bolt to strike me.

"Freya…" I warn.

"What do you want me to say, Luca? I thought you'd hang up. Actually, I thought you wouldn't answer."

I rear back, shocked at how much her words sting. I open my mouth to tell her that I'll always answer her call, but then a bolt of lightning splits the sky open, followed immediately by a deafening clap of thunder. The next thing I know, Freya is in my arms, clinging to me with all her might.

My arms wrap around her as she buries her face into my chest, trying to muffle her cries. She's shaking so badly I think she might pass out on me. Whatever is going on, it's not a game to her. Freya is fucking terrified, and like me, her anxiety is coming out as anger and frustration.

I hold her tightly and press my lips onto the crown of her head, breathing in her lavender and saltwater scent. We stay locked in each other's embrace for long moments until Freya finally untangles herself from me.

She grabs her purse and looks up at me, her beautiful green eyes rimmed in red and glistening with tears. We don't speak, but I take her hand and guide her outside, pausing briefly so she can lock her door. I wrap my arm around her shoulders and lead her to my recklessly parked vehicle.

Twenty minutes later, Freya is set up in one of my guest rooms with Larry, Curly, and Mo snuggled up all around her. It's not the first time I've been jealous of the cute little bastards, and I get the feeling it won't be the last.

As much as I want to curl up behind her, I don't want to push her too far tonight. God knows what's going on in Freya's head right now. The last thing I want to do is crowd her or make her uncomfortable. I'll have to settle for the fact that she's under my roof. I'll also have to settle for the fact that I won't be able to sleep for the rest of the night. All in all, a small price to pay for Freya's safety.

I managed to get a few hours of restless sleep, but I woke with a start around five-thirty this morning. I've been in my home office for three hours now, getting some things done so I can clear out the rest of the day for whatever is going on with Freya.

Yesterday I was okay with letting her give me answers in her own time, but after last night, I need to know what the fuck has her so scared. This is not the fiery, outgoing, bold woman who stormed into my life a few months ago. And I don't like it.

"You look so dapper in your new collar, Mo!" I hear Freya coo from the guest room across the hall from my office. "Did you know your daddy picked it out for you?"

I roll my eyes at her referring to me as a dad to these animals, but secretly, I don't hate it. As if I needed any more proof this woman has me by the balls.

"Ready to go outside, Larry and Curly?" The two dogs bark excitedly, followed by a sad whining noise from Mo. "Mo, honey, why don't you try using the litter box?" The spoiled cat meows angrily, making Freya laugh. "Alright, outside with all three of you, then. I better see you do your business, Mo. We can't have you peeing all over Luca's things and making him regret taking you in."

I hope she knows I wouldn't toss any of the Stooges out. How could I? She clearly loves them, and I'm resigned to the fact that I'd pretty much do anything to see her happy.

While Freya takes the little monsters outside, I finish up with the last of my work and head to the kitchen to see what I can find for breakfast. Only when I hear the clicking of Larry and Curly's nails on the hardwood floor, do I turn around.

Freya is standing in the doorway of my kitchen, wearing nothing but the t-shirt I gave her last night. Her clothes were soaking wet by the time we got back to my place, and we left her apartment without packing any of her things. The shirt is huge on her, hitting just above her knees. It's not indecent at all, but fuck if the sight of her in my clothes doesn't have my dick surging to life.

"Morning," I grunt, turning away from her so I can adjust myself discreetly.

"Morning. Where's the dog food? I can feed the dogs while you feed us?"

"I'll feed you something alright," I mutter to myself.

"Hmm?"

I clear my throat and try to get my thoughts under control. I need answers, not to get my dick sucked.

"You like bacon and eggs?" I ask instead of answering her.

"I'm pretty sure it's unconstitutional to dislike bacon. Anyone who says they don't like it is lying. Even if they are morally against eating animals, they still have to concede that bacon is fucking delicious."

I grin at her answer. I shouldn't be surprised she has strong opinions about breakfast food. The woman has strong opinions about everything.

Freya gets to work feeding the Three Stooges while I serve up our very constitutional breakfast. We eat in silence, both of us lost in our thoughts. I'm about to ask if she was able to get to sleep last night, just to have something to break the weird tension, but she speaks up first.

"So, thanks for last night. Like I said, I was just being a chicken shit."

"That doesn't sound like you."

"What?"

"You're not a chicken shit. Tell me what's really going on."

"The storm —"

"And the parking lot? It wasn't thundering then."

"I was overreac —"

"Freya. I seriously hope you don't think you can lie to me. I've become quite well-versed in reading people, and while you're not a chicken shit, you are full of shit right now."

She huffs out a breath and crunches down on a piece of bacon. If I weren't so frustrated with trying to get the truth out of her, I'd take the time to appreciate how adorable she is when she's annoyed with me.

I wait her out, never looking away from her. Freya squirms a bit in her chair and then sighs heavily.

"Fine, okay, so my dad wasn't a great guy or whatever. He gambled, drank, slept around, did his fair share of drugs. Obviously, that caused some money problems." Freya refuses to look at me, choosing instead to push the scrambled eggs around on her plate with a fork.

She furrows her brow and purses her lips as if trying to find the right words before continuing. "It's a cliché story, really. Desperate man gets a loan from sketchy people, can't pay it back, gets another loan to pay off the first one, can't pay it back, rinse and repeat until things snowball out of control and the forgotten daughter ends up in foster care."

If I didn't already know her father was dead, I'd put a bullet between his eyes myself. I know what addicts do when they are backed into a corner, and Freya doesn't deserve any of that. I can't say for sure if he was abusive, but it wouldn't surprise me. At the very least, he was neglectful.

I nod my head slowly, even though Freya still isn't looking at me. "You think some of these sketchy people are following you? After all this time?"

"Something like that," she murmurs, shrugging her shoulders.

"What aren't you telling me, baby?"

Freya's wide eyes dart up to mine, seemingly as shocked at my term of endearment for her as I am. Why did I call her that? And why does it feel so right?

"Nothing. It doesn't matter. You asked why I freaked out in the parking lot and during the storm, and that's why, okay? I didn't say it made any sense or that it's a legitimate concern," she spits out. Freya is putting on her armor piece by piece, protecting her surprisingly tender heart from me.

I know my window of opportunity to get her to open up to me is quickly closing. If I want her trust, I have to give her mine in return. Freya gave me pieces of her past, and it's only fair that I give her a few pieces of mine.

I clear my throat and tell her something only Matteo knows about me.

"I left home at thirteen and spent three years living on the streets."

Chapter 8

Freya

Luca's confession throws me completely off guard. I reach out and rest my hand over his, needing to comfort him in some way. I need to comfort me, too, seeing as his words tore my freaking heart in two. I know what it's like to be homeless. It's not something I would ever wish upon anyone, especially the complicated, endearing, confusing, and surprisingly sweet man in front of me.

"My *mamma* was a first-generation Italian immigrant. She came here to America with my dad, who left her as soon as he found out she was pregnant. After that, *mamma* had a string of nameless, faceless asshole boyfriends who came and went. Let's just say I learned how to defend myself pretty early on in life."

I squeeze his hand, encouraging him to continue. Luca looks down at our entwined hands with that same expression he had before we kissed. He's studying me, memorizing me, trying to figure out whatever the hell is going on between us. I have no idea what this connection is, but it's clear I'm not the only one feeling it.

Luca gently rubs his thumb over my knuckles, like he's drawing strength from my touch. It makes me feel powerful and important, the fact that I have something this man needs.

"The last guy she was with was a real piece of work. Allen," he growls the name and squeezes my hand tightly. I feel the rage coursing through him, and I just want to make it go away. I squeeze his hand right back, which makes him loosen his grip once again. "Sorry," he murmurs, turning my hand over as if inspecting it for damage. Luca pauses when he sees the marks I've made from digging my nails into my palm. He traces over them in the most tender of touches, but he doesn't ask how I got them.

"I'm okay," I promise. "Tell me more."

Luca sighs, looking up at me with conflicted blue eyes. He nods and looks away from me again like he doesn't want to see my reaction to whatever he's going to tell me next.

"Allen was a degenerate motherfucker, probably not unlike your dad. He was a mean, abusive drunk with more addictions and vices than anyone I've ever met. Late one night, I heard him and my mom fighting, which wasn't that uncommon. But then I heard a scream and a loud crash, followed by a chilling silence. I snuck out of bed and carefully made my way towards the main room of our trailer, where I found my mom lying on the floor in a pool of blood."

"Oh my God, Luca…"

"Allen had his back turned towards me, and I didn't have time to think about what I did next. I grabbed the gun he always left lying around and took my shot. The dumb bastard didn't even have the safety on."

"Did you…"

"Yeah. He was my first kill. I've never regretted it." His words are colder now, detached. I get it. Sometimes the only way to come back from those memories is to distance yourself, pretend it's not really your life, it's someone else's, and you're just telling their story.

"Anyway," he continues. "I left that night. Packed up whatever I could and walked out, leaving the two of them bleeding out in the shitty trailer park on the southside. I knew the cops wouldn't spend the resources to figure out who shot Allen in the back of the head. We were trailer trash, all of us, so who cared what happened to two deadbeat junkies?"

I swallow back tears for all the pain Luca had to deal with at such an early age. I understand it on a soul-deep level. The toxic family, the need to escape, ending up on the streets. Everything in me hates that he dealt with all of that in his past, but in a totally fucked-up way, I feel closer to him than ever, even if he doesn't know it.

"So, that's how I ended up homeless at thirteen. Matteo caught me stealing money from one of the bookies for the Moscatelli family when I was sixteen. Instead of killing me like I thought he would, he took me in, told me to get my GED, and then offered me a job. Fast forward almost twenty years, and here we are."

He shrugs, still not looking up at me. I lean forward, reaching out to cup the side of his face, melting a little more for him when he leans into my touch.

"You're a fucking warrior," I whisper. "And you should be proud of how far you've come." Luca finally meets my gaze. He swallows hard as he stares down into the very depths of who I am and lets me do the same to him.

"How do you do that?" He murmurs.

"Do what?"

"You...I don't like to be touched."

I immediately withdraw my hand, but he grabs it and brings it up to his mouth, placing the softest kiss on my palm, right over the half-moon marks before resting it on his cheek again.

"I don't like to be touched by anyone but you. Growing up with my mom and her boyfriends, and then being homeless...I don't know. I'm fucked up. Never had any good come from someone's touch, but then you..."

I close the distance between us and kiss the incredible, vulnerable, strong man in front of me, because how could I not? Luca parts his lips, allowing me to slide my tongue inside his mouth. I whimper softly as I pour out every unnamed emotion, drinking his down as well.

Luca deepens the kiss, pulling me onto his lap so I'm straddling him. I feel his hands everywhere, sliding under the shirt I'm wearing, caressing my back, my hips, my thighs. His large, calloused fingers roam over my skin in the lightest of touches, and then dig into my flesh, rocking me against his hardening cock.

"Fuck," he grunts into the side of my neck before kissing me there. "You're so fucking soft," he groans, trailing more kisses down my neck and shoulder.

Luca stands up abruptly, keeping me in his arms as he turns and sets me down on the table. I squeal at the sudden movement, but he captures the sound in his mouth, sucking all the air out of my lungs in a punishing, devastating kiss.

He grips my inner thighs and spreads my legs apart so he can get closer to my aching core. Luca grinds his thick dick against me and tangles his fingers in my hair, ripping my mouth away from his and nipping at my jaw.

A shiver runs through me when he covers the little bite with a sweet kiss. He's dominant, demanding, and territorial, while also being tender and caring. It's addictive, the way he handles me. A girl could get used to this.

"Need to taste more of you, *la mia anima*."

I'm so lost in the way his cock is rubbing against my throbbing clit, I hardly register his words. I nod my head, knowing I'll like whatever Luca does next.

To my complete shock, Luca grips the neckline of the shirt I'm wearing and tears it in two. I gasp and giggle at his eagerness, but then moan when I feel his tongue circling my nipple. Luca grunts and licks the other one before closing his lips around it and sucking. Hard.

I squeeze my thighs around his hips and lean back on my hands, giving him more access. His hands and mouth cover every inch of my breasts and torso with kisses, bites, pinches, and soothing strokes.

I've always been a bigger girl, and I've grown to love my curves, but that doesn't mean I don't struggle with body image from time to time. Especially when I'm in the presence of a freaking ripped god of a man. But Luca doesn't leave any space for self-doubt. It's clear he likes what he sees. What he feels. What he tastes.

Luca scrapes his teeth down my soft belly and kneels in front of me, shouldering my knees apart so he's staring right at my panty-covered pussy. I know he sees how shamefully wet I am. How wet he's made me. Luca leans forward and covers the wet spot with his mouth, sucking on the fabric and making me gasp in surprise.

He grunts into my pussy and breathes in deep. Holy hell, this man is fucking hot. Everything he does. Knowing I'm the only one he wants to touch, the only one he wants to touch him makes this all so much more than incredibly erotic. It's deeper, more meaningful. It's everything.

Luca hooks his thumbs into the side of my panties and slowly drags them down my legs until I'm bare before him. For a few seconds, he just stares at me. It's unnerving. No one has ever seen me like this. Touched me like this. Ruined me like this.

I feel him pepper kisses up the insides of my thighs, first one, and then the other. Then he parts my lips with his thumbs and lets out a strangled moan.

"Jesus Christ, you're dripping for me. I need it. Need to taste it. Need to." He sounds like a man possessed. I love it. How am I the one doing this to him? Why me?

I don't have time to overthink it before his tongue is sliding through my folds. I gasp and moan, falling backward onto the table. Luca licks me up and down, humming into my pussy like it's the best thing he's ever tasted. I swear I feel his wet, hot tongue deep in my core, the liquid heat pooling inside me and filling my veins with burning ecstasy.

Luca leans back slightly, and I whimper at the loss of him. Then he swipes two fingers up my slit, pulling my pussy lips open and forming a cage around my clit with his fingers. My eyes slam shut as his tongue makes contact with my isolated bundle of nerves.

The whole world zooms down to just Luca and me. He sucks down on me fiercely and I feel my body wind up fast and hard. When I'm about to come, he backs away and pushes his tongue inside of me, lapping at my throbbing channel. One finger finds my clit and he brushes it softly, never letting me go over the edge but making sure I'm still right there.

"Please, please…" I whine, squirming beneath him and trying to get him where I need him most.

Luca ignores me, continuing to torture my swollen, sensitive cunt with his tongue. I feel his finger circling my entrance, over and over, then dipping inside. I moan, feeling my tight channel stretch around his large digit. Fuck, I can't even imagine what his cock is going to feel like. I don't know if I'll survive, but I sure as hell want to try.

He slowly works his finger in and out of me with gentle thrusts, then he curls it up. Holy. Fucking. Shit. My body spasms violently, causing my thighs to close around his head and my back to bow off the table.

"That feels good?" He asks, his voice low and gravelly, sending another shiver up my spine.

"So…good…" I gasp.

Luca makes that same sound in the back of his throat like he did the other day. It's a grunt of acknowledgment like he's confirming a suspicion. He curls his finger up again and rubs that spot, then taps it over and over.

"Luca! Luca...I..."

He fingerfucks me hard and sucks on my clit, growling into my pussy. My muscles lock up tight, each thrust and rough lick sending me higher, higher, higher...

And then I shatter.

I scream out his name and claw at the table as my orgasm ravishes me. Luca slides his hands underneath my ass and pulls me closer, burying his face into my pulsing cunt and drinking down all of my release. I squeeze my eyes shut and fall into pleasure so intense I think I might pass out.

"You're okay, baby. I've got you."

I open my eyes, noticing I'm on the couch, curled up in Luca's lap. "I... What?"

He chuckles softly, the hearty sound traveling through my body, warming up my bones. I've never heard him laugh, so this feels huge. I hope to hear a real, unfiltered laugh sometime. I want to give him that.

"I lost you there for a minute. I take it you were pleased?" He's smirking at me, which is another first that I absolutely adore, but there's a hint of doubt in his eyes.

"I am very pleased," I grin back at him. "Pleased and weak and worn out. I mean...fuck, Luca. That was..." I shake my head, not able to find the words in my scrambled brain to even describe it.

"Yeah, it really was."

Luca kisses me sweetly on the lips and then on my forehead. I never thought I could feel this safe, this cherished, this well taken care of. And I certainly didn't expect Luca to be the one to make me feel this way.

Our tender, confusing moment is interrupted by Luca's phone ringing.

"Goddamnit," he mutters. I see indecision in his beautiful blue eyes, but in the end, he kisses me one last time and sets me down on the couch before walking over to where his phone is sitting on the counter. "What?" He barks. His jaw tenses as a low growl rumbles through his chest. "Fuck." His eyes tick over to mine, and I know what he's about to say. "Yeah, I'll be there soon."

It shouldn't hurt as much as it does that he's leaving. It's not like he's kicking me out or something. But after all of the emotional confessions and then the truly life-altering orgasm, I can't help but feel a little rejected.

Before he can see any of those feelings on my face, I hop up and make my way to the guest bedroom, where Luca set out my clothes from the night before after washing and drying them. I don't get very far, however. Luca wraps his arm around my waist and pulls me into his side, all while listening to whoever is on the other end of the call.

He grunts his goodbye and then tosses his phone on the couch before turning towards me and kissing me until my lips are bruised and we're both panting for air.

"I fucking hate to leave you," he murmurs, his lips pressed against my temple.

"I'm not a huge fan of it either," I sigh.

"The sooner I go, the sooner I'll be back. I just have to take care of a few things. Stay here."

"Um..."

"Stay here," he says again, his voice harder this time. I don't want to argue with him, for once in my life, so I just nod my head. "Good. That's settled."

Luca untangles himself from me, giving me one last kiss on the forehead, and then heads off towards his room to change. Ten minutes later, he's dressed in his standard three-piece suit that looks sexy as fuck on him. I managed to put on my pajama shorts and ratty t-shirt from last night, sans panties, since I have no idea where he flung them.

I suddenly feel unworthy and out of place. Sure, Luca came from nothing, but he's made something of himself. He's respected, revered, and in control at all times.

Me, on the other hand, not so much. I'm still a mess. I may project an air of confidence, but truthfully, I still feel like a scared little girl most of the time. I don't belong in his world any more than he belongs in mine.

"See you soon, baby girl," he says on his way out the door. I nod and give him my best smile, not wanting him to know what I'm thinking.

A feeling of emptiness hits me as soon as I hear the door click shut. I take the dogs outside one last time and fill up their food bowls before ordering an Uber to pick me up a few blocks away. I know he's going to be pissed, but I need some space. I need to figure my shit out. I need to find a way to be worthy of him.

Chapter 9

Luca

"Are we done here?" I grunt at Rocco, our top enforcer.

He gives me some strong side-eye, but then looks away when I glare at him. My patience left me about twenty minutes into this fucking mess of a situation. I had hoped to come in, question the little fucker who thought he could skim off the top of one of our shipments of drugs, and call it a day.

Instead, the interrogation turned into a whole fucking ordeal. After consulting with Matteo, who was not pleased to be interrupted during his honeymoon, Rocco and I gathered up a bunch of other little fucks who were getting greedy, and...took care of them.

It took us all fucking day. Eight excruciating hours. Eight hours away from Freya's juicy cunt, soft curves, round ass, and pink, hard little nipples. Eight hours away from her sassy little mouth and her tender heart. Eight hours away from the woman who shattered everything I thought I knew about myself and then rebuilt me with her soft words, gentle touch, and sexy fucking body.

Jesus Christ. I've never gone down on a woman before, for obvious reasons, but now I'm addicted. Only Freya. Only she could bring me to my knees – literally. One taste and I knew. I knew I could live there, between her thick thighs and tight little pussy, dripping, and pulsing with need.

Feeling, licking, tasting the soft, slick skin between her legs was a high like nothing I've ever experienced. Discovering what made her whimper, what made her moan, what made her scream and spasm and shoot her cream into my mouth, was one of the greatest pleasures I've ever experienced. And I didn't even come.

My dick is angry at me. He has been all day. I fucking *need* to be inside her. It's not just about getting off, though. I need to feel the very depths of her, fill her up with my cock, my cum, my goddamn soul I didn't know I had until Freya showed up in my life.

"Luca? Yo, what is up with you today? You're as bad as Matteo was. Wait, holy shit, don't tell me some chick is messing with your head, too."

I growl at Rocco, but the stupid ass smirk doesn't leave his face. "She's not some chick."

"I'll take that as a yes," he says, his smirk turning into a cocky grin.

"Keep it up. You'll get knocked on your ass by a woman one of these days," I grumble.

"Me? Nah, I ain't about that life. Women are nothing but trouble."

"Maybe. But the right one is worth it."

He just shakes his head at me and packs up his interrogation tools. "We're done here. You can go on back to your little distraction."

I can't help the small little grin that spreads across my lips. Freya is a distraction. The best distraction. And she wants *me* for some reason. She finds me worthy to touch her, taste her, see her laid out before me. Fuck if that doesn't make me puff out my chest with pride.

"Keep giving me shit, Rocco. I'm going to enjoy watching you fall head over heels one of these days."

"Not gonna happen," he grunts, making his way towards the door leading upstairs.

"Yeah, I thought the same thing," I mutter to myself, knowing Rocco can't hear me.

Twenty minutes later, I'm pulling up to my house. I practically leap out of my car, eager to pick up where we left off. I hope she's not pissed at me for being gone so long. I thought about texting or calling her, but I didn't want to seem desperate. I feel like I'm a kid who has his first crush. I guess in a way, I kind of am. I've never felt anything remotely close to what I feel for Freya.

I burst through the front door, feeling like a beast who needs to devour its prey. I need to get my shit together before I scare Freya off. I've never been this desperate for someone and it's fucking with me.

The Three Stooges come running up to me, begging for some attention. Even with their excited whimpers and clacking of nails as they jump and wiggle around, my house feels empty. She's not here. I feel it. Or rather, I don't feel it. I don't feel her presence. I scoop Larry and Curly up and walk through the house, with Mo trailing contentedly behind me.

"Freya?" I call out, hoping like hell I'm wrong.

I tear through the rooms in my house, cursing the fact that there are so many. I know she's not here, but I have to check everywhere.

What the fuck? Did something happen to her? Did the fuckers she's scared of find her? Fear grips my heart, and I scramble for my phone, fumbling with it and dropping it on the floor.

"Goddamnit!" I roar. The dogs shy away from me, and I feel like a dick. "Sorry," I mutter, shaking my head again at the man I've become. Apologizing to dogs. Worrying about the woman who used to drive me crazy. Well, she still drives me crazy, but for entirely different reasons.

I pick up my phone and head towards the back door, letting the dogs, and the cat who thinks he's a dog, outside.

"Hey," comes the sweet voice on the other end of the line. I take a breath for what feels like the first time since I got home. Relief washes over me, making me light-headed. But then it turns to anger.

"Where the fuck are you?" I growl.

"Woah, calm down there. I'm at home."

"No, you're not," I grunt.

"What?"

I think I shocked myself as much as I shocked her. This is her home. I am her home. And she's not with me, which pisses me right the fuck off.

"I told you to stay here." The words sound gruff, even to my own ears.

So much for not scaring her away, asshole.

"I'm not a dog, you can't just command me to do shit."

"I know you're not a dog. My dogs listen to me," I grumble.

Freya snorts out a laugh, which annoys me, frustrates me, and settles something deep inside. She's okay. She's pushing all of my buttons right now, but she's safe. Though not as safe as she should be. I hate how easy it would be for someone to break in, and I really hate that she's clearly afraid of someone and still staying there alone.

"Luca, listen. I just need some time to process all of this."

I barely hear her words as I let the dogs in and then rush outside and hop into my car. "Fine. Process away. You have ten minutes, then I'm coming for you, baby." I hang up before she can argue.

Chapter 10

Luca

I'm at her place in eight minutes, going twice as fast as the legal limit for the second time in less than twenty-four hours. I sprint up to her door, banging on it with enough force to rattle the damn thing on its hinges.

I hear a frustrated sigh on the other side of the door, and then it swings open, revealing a beautiful, angry Freya. I can't stop myself as I grab her face in my hands and crash my mouth down on hers.

She may be pissed, but she parts her lips for me as I walk her backward into her apartment, kicking the door shut with my foot and pressing her up against the wall. I grab both her wrists and pin them above her head before swallowing down her fight and fury.

Freya tears her mouth away from mine, causing me to growl and pull at her bottom lip with my teeth.

"Don't ever leave me again," I murmur into the side of her neck, biting her there and then licking away the sting. "I can give you space, as long as I'm sharing that space with you."

She laughs, though it comes out all breathy and sexy as fuck. "I think that's the opposite of giving me space."

I take a deep breath and summon up all of my willpower, then take a step back, releasing her wrists. I drop my gaze down her body, then look away as I bare my heart to her once more.

"I want you to process whatever you need to process. I know it's a lot. It's confusing for me too, but there's no denying what's between us. I can't fucking think without you, I feel like I can't breathe if we're not sharing the same air. I don't want to be overbearing, but Jesus, just...please don't ever leave me."

I can't look at her knowing I just ripped my goddamn chest open, for the second time today, I might add. Then I feel her hand cupping the side of my face, her thumb stroking the light stubble on my jaw.

"I feel like I can't breathe without you, either. And I'm scared."

My eyes lock on hers, searching those clear green irises for all the things she's not telling me.

"You're scared of me?"

"No. Yes. No, not *you* specifically. I'm scared to need you the way I do. I'm scared I'm not..." She sighs heavily and drops her hand from my face. Freya wraps her arms around her middle like she's trying to protect herself from me. I hate it.

"You're not what?" I whisper, wanting like hell to pull her into my arms, but knowing she needs this moment to wrestle with her thoughts on her own. I stand in front of her, still caging her in against the wall, but not touching her.

"Not enough," she whispers.

I reach out and cup the back of her neck, gently drawing her closer to me so I can rest my forehead on hers. "Freya, you are everything. I'm no good at this shit. I don't know what I'm doing, I just know that you broke me, and I need you to put me back together."

She gasps and leans back, staring right at me with tears in her eyes. I lean down and take her lips in a soft kiss, letting her taste my truth and begging her without words to show me her truth, too.

Freya glides her hands up my chest and shoulders, sliding my jacket off in one swift motion. I groan into her hot little mouth and slip my hands under the hem of her tank top, tugging it up and over her head. A deep growl rumbles through my chest when I see she doesn't have a bra on.

"You got to take a piece of clothing off me, it's only fair I get to do the same."

"But you have so much more clothing on than me. I'll be naked before I even get to see any of you."

"Lucky me, then."

I take her lips in a frantic kiss as she works at the buttons of my vest and shirt. I want her hands on me right this fucking second. I lean back and rip my shirt off, sending buttons flying all around us. Freya giggles then leans forward and licks a path up the center of my chest.

"Fuck, do it again," I demand, already working on my belt. Her tongue feels incredible on my skin. I never knew pleasure like this existed, and I haven't even been inside of her yet.

Freya licks my chest again, this time swiping her tongue over one nipple and then the other. I growl and push her back against the wall before dropping to my knees, pulling her leggings and panties down as I go.

"Need to taste you again. I want your sweet cream on my tongue when I fuck you."

"Luca…" she moans, leaning against the wall and tangling her fingers in my hair.

I pause for a moment, getting my carnal obsession under control. She just told me she needed space and here I am, ripping her clothes off, ready to claim that cherry I know she saved just for me. "Do you want that?"

Freya looks down at me and bites her lip. I see her warring with herself, desire and lust battling it out with doubts and insecurities. I pepper a line of kisses from one hip to her other hip, giving her time to decide what she wants while still teasing her. I'll wait if that's what she wants, but I'm still going to give her a mind-blowing orgasm. I don't even care if I get stuck with another case of painful blue balls as long as I give her pleasure.

My hands slide up and down the back of her legs, my fingers trailing up the insides of her thighs, closer, closer, closer to her wet heat.

"Tell me what you want. Anything. I'll give it to you. I'll lay the whole damn world at your feet," I murmur into the little patch of soft curls covering her mound. Before she can answer, I dip my tongue into her folds, growling as her sweet, tangy flavor hits my tongue.

I lick her from bottom to top, swirling the tip of my tongue around her clit. This may only be my second time doing this, but I'm a quick learner. I know what she likes, and I'll spend the rest of my life discovering what other pleasures I can bring her.

"Fuck, Luca," she moans. "How am I supposed to think when your tongue is doing such wicked things to me?"

"How am I supposed to think *without* my tongue doing such wicked things to you?" I counter.

She laughs, the motion causing her cunt to contract and release more of her sticky juices. I lean down and suck on her pussy lips, then drag my tongue all around her folds, dipping in and out of every crease, taking note of the places that make her moan and tremble.

She's almost there. I can taste it. Her needy little pussy clenches up and her muscles tense. Freya fists my hair and shoves me further in between her thighs, but I pull back.

"Wh-what?" She asks through the cloud of lust surrounding her.

"Tell me what you want."

"I..."

I lick her slit just once, loving the way her body twitches when I circle my tongue around her clit.

"Tell me, baby girl. What do you want?"

"I want..."

I hear the strain in her voice. I know what she wants, and I know she knows what she wants. Freya's just too damn stubborn to admit it. That's okay. I can be stubborn too. I wrap my lips around her throbbing clit and suck, pulling the little bundle of nerves in between my lips and then grazing my teeth over it.

"Oh fuck," she whimpers. "Fuck, fuck, fuck, yes. I want this, I want you, I want you, I want you," she chants over and over as her orgasm rips through her. I suck down her release and catch her as her knees give out. I cradle her in my arms and kiss her forehead as she pants for air and comes down from her high.

"You have me, *la mia anima.* I'm yours."

"Mine," she whispers, tracing a finger down my nose and over my lips.

I stand up and carry her over to her bed, which is far too small for both of us. It will have to do for now. There's no way I can wait until we get home to have her. This is what we need. I may not have a ton of experience, but I know I can please my woman. I know I can show her what it means to belong to me, how well we fit together, how she'll never have this connection with anyone except me.

I set her down on the twin mattress and get to work on tearing the rest of my clothes off. I'm so caught up in the way she's staring at me with her gorgeous green eyes, that I forget all about my shoes. Freya giggles, making her large breasts shake. I growl and kick my shoes off before yanking the rest of my clothes off my body, fisting my cock as soon as the angry fucker springs free.

Freya sits up on her knees and reaches out for me, placing her palms on my bare chest. I close my eyes and tilt my head back, pumping my swollen dick while she takes her time exploring me, exploring what belongs to her.

Freya drags one hand down my abs, lower, fuck, lower, until she's gripping my cock, taking over for me.

"Jesus," I grit out, snapping my eyes open and looking down at her little hand that can barely fit around me. "Baby, I'm gonna need you to stop if you want this to last longer than ten seconds."

Freya gasps in surprise then bites her bottom lip and gives me a devious smile. Then the little minx bends down and sucks my cock into her mouth, swirling her tongue around the tip and licking up the steady stream of precum pouring out of me.

I can't stop my hips from bucking and my hands gripping the sides of her head, holding her steady while I ease my way in and out of her mouth.

"Gotta stop, baby. Gotta pull back," I growl, though I can't seem to let her go. I finally pry my hands away from her, groaning when she releases my dick from her mouth with a pop.

I push her back onto the mattress and climb on top of her, immediately seeking out her lips and spearing my tongue inside her mouth. I don't give a fuck that I taste myself on her. In fact, it makes me feel like a fucking king that this goddess sucked my cock and now wants me inside of her.

"Please," she whispers, spreading her legs wider for me and tilting her hips so my hard, heavy length settles in between her warm, wet folds.

I begin thrusting up and down her slit, gathering up her juices and letting them coat my cock. Leaning down, I brush my nose along her neck and then kiss her lips softly. "This is your first time, right, baby girl?"

"Yeah," she whispers, searing me with her intense green eyes. I look for any hints of doubt or fear, but I only see lust. Lust and a longing that matches my own. She wants to be filled as much as I want to fill her, and not just physically. She wants more. And I want to give her everything.

"I've only ever been with one person," I confess, burying my face into the side of her neck so I don't have to look at her. I feel like she needs to know about my history, too. "It was just once. I was young, I wanted to know what it felt like. I wish I waited for you. This is the experience I want, not some fling, not some experiment. Just you. Only you. All of you."

I kiss her pulse point, which is pounding rapidly against my lips. "Luca," she whispers. "Let me be your first too. Let me experience it all with you."

I lift my head up and look at her, my beautiful goddess, my savior, my infuriating, complicated, dream woman. I rest my forehead on hers and line myself up with her entrance, pushing just the tip inside.

Freya squeezes her eyes shut, and I kiss her closed eyelids. "Look at me, *la mia anima*. Look at me while I claim you once and for all."

Her eyes pop open and I slide another inch inside of her tight, sopping wet channel. Freya whimpers and digs her fingernails into my shoulders. I stop, not wanting to hurt her, but Freya surprises the fuck out of me by bucking her hips and shoving her pussy further down my cock.

"Yessss…" She moans.

"Fuck, little girl. Look at you, so eager for my dick. This what you need?" I pull back and push inside of her again, going a little deeper this time until I reach her barrier. She tenses in my arms, but then nods her head, wiggling her hips and making me lose my goddamn mind.

"You. You are what I need."

That's it. I snap my hips forward, tearing through her innocence and fucking claiming this cunt as my new home.

"Mine," I growl as I bury myself deep inside of her. Freya whimpers and locks her ankles behind my back holding me close.

"Yes, I need it, I need it," she whispers over and over. I stay still, letting us both feel this connection for the first time.

My cock twitches and leaks more precum, but I grit my teeth and hold back my orgasm, waiting until she loosens up and gets used to my size.

"Move!" She demands, making me chuckle. Freya moans as the laughter rolls through my body, the vibrations making her already wet pussy absolutely drenched for me.

I pull back and stare down between us, savoring her creamy white cum mixed with my own and the evidence of her virginity. Christ, I almost fall right off the edge at the sight. I fill her up again, slowly working my cock in and out of her pussy, growling at the way her walls suck me in and pulse around me.

Freya grips the back of my neck and pulls me down for a frantic kiss while circling her hips and meeting me thrust for thrust. I hook my hand under her right knee and pull her leg up and to the side, opening her up even more and switching up the angle.

I know there's a spot inside of her that drives her wild, I just need to find it again. I thrust back inside in long, rough strokes, scraping my cock along her walls in search of her secret little treasure.

"Oh fuck, Jesus Christ, holy shit!" Freya cries out.

"There it is," I grunt, hammering into that spot.

"Luca! I can't, I can't, I..." She shakes and tenses and gasps for air, but I don't let up. I keep striking that same spot, over and over, so hard I'm pushing her up the mattress with each vicious stroke. Some part of me knows I should slow down, be gentle with her since it's her first time, but fuck, looking at her face twisted up in pleasure makes me drive into her harder, faster, giving her more, needing more for myself.

"Come for me, Freya. Let go," I groan, dipping my head to suck on her bouncing tits.

"I want to, I want to, I-I w-want..."

"Do it!" I growl, rearing back and throwing her legs over my shoulders. I pound that little pussy over and over, groaning along with her as she squeezes me so goddamn tight.

Freya claws at my chest and screams out her orgasm. She's absolutely ruined, coming apart beneath me, squirming and tensing and trying to get away from this intense pleasure. I hold her in place, making her feel all of it, every single second.

Before she has a chance to recover, I pull out of her and grip her hips, flipping her around and positioning her on her hands and knees.

"Fuck," I groan, sliding my hands up and down her back and then squeezing the soft flesh of her ass. I pull her cheeks apart and slam my thick dick into her pulsing little pussy, growling at the sloppy wet sounds we're making as I fuck my woman hard and fast.

She moans and arches her back, wedging my cock deeper inside of her. "I'm so close already, I'm so close…"

I lean over her, covering her entire body with my large frame. I rest my hands on top of hers, caging her in and lacing our fingers together while I grind my cock into her swollen, beat-up little pussy.

"Harder, please, so fucking hard…so good, please."

Her desperate cries have my balls drawing up tight as fire races through my veins. "Whatever you want, my queen. I'll give you everything."

I rut into her, tearing her cunt apart. Freya throws her head back, resting it on my shoulder. I turn my head and suck on her neck, holding still inside of her as she comes. It's quiet and brutal, the way her release overwhelms her.

Feeling her orgasm pulse around my dick is incredible. I fuck her through it, so damn hard, as she sobs beneath me and soaks my cock. The bed creaks and the headboard slams against the wall, but I can't stop.

Freya screams and comes again, taking me with her. Just as my orgasm hits, the bed frame cracks, and the mattress drops to the floor. I collapse on top of her, holding myself deep inside as the last of my cum shoots out of my dick.

We lie there, a sweaty, tangled mess, until I eventually roll to the side. I drape Freya's limp body over my chest and wrap my arms around her, tucking her head under my chin.

"You okay?" I whisper, kissing the top of her head.

"Holy fuck," she breathes out, making me laugh. "Do that again," she says.

"Do what again? Fuck you? Give me a few minutes," I chuckle.

"No, I mean...laugh. I like your laugh." I freeze at her words and swallow down the lump in my throat. "But yeah, you can fuck me again, too," she sighs, snuggling deeper into my chest.

"I think I can arrange both of those things. I told you I'd give you whatever you want."

"Mmmm," she hums contentedly. I stroke her back and play with her wild, messy hair. I love knowing I caused her red curls to tangle and stick to the back of her sweaty neck. I love knowing I'm the one who made her sweat, made her come, again and again. Fucking hell, I'm almost ready to go again.

But I didn't plan on coming over here to ravish her. I came to talk. Not that I'm complaining.

"Stay with me," I whisper, too afraid to say it louder.

"I can't," she shakes her head and nuzzles her face into the side of my neck. There's no conviction behind her protest, though. She wants to. She wants me to convince her, to fight for her. Challenge accepted.

"You can. The dogs miss you."

"The dogs, huh?" She pushes up on my chest, looking down at me with the cutest smile on her face. "I'm pretty sure I just saw them this morning."

"Well, I missed you and you saw me this morning. So, it's not totally ridiculous to assume the little mutts miss you, too."

"Hey! Larry, Curly, and Mo are not mutts! They're my family!" She says indignantly, but playfully at the same time.

I pull her down for a kiss, because fuck it, she's that damn irresistible all the time. "Our family," I whisper into her parted lips before kissing her again.

Freya pulls back and looks at me intently like she's picking apart my words and testing to see if they're true or not. With a little nod of her head, I know I've passed her test.

"Fine, but I'll need to pack up a few things. Do you have space for another desktop computer?"

"What?" I laugh, then look around and see a massive computer tower, two screens, and a laptop set up in the corner of the room. How the hell did I miss that before? "What is all that for?"

Freya sighs and lays back down, settling her chin on my chest so she can look up at me. I tilt my head and hold her gaze, waiting for her to tell me another one of her secrets.

"Okay, so maybe I have a side hustle. Or like, a full-time hustle with brief side hustles like working at the animal shelter or the bath bomb store."

"And what exactly is this full-time hustle?" I ask with genuine curiosity.

"I'm sort of a hacker."

I'm stunned at first, but then a deep laugh rolls through me, starting in my gut and working its way through my chest and out of my mouth. I throw my head back and let it consume me. Fuck, I've never felt this good.

I'm laughing so hard I feel Freya bounce up and down on my chest. She joins me, giggling and then hugging me. This is the best moment of my life. I want to have this every single day for as long as I live.

"Of course, you are," I say once I've calmed down a bit. "You are sexy, sassy, and incredibly smart and resourceful. You're the full package, my little criminal mastermind."

Freya giggles again, the sound sinking into every part of me and filling me up with light. "You're one to talk, Mr. Mafia Man," she sasses.

"We're going to make an excellent power couple," I murmur, pulling her in for another kiss. Freya sighs and curls up on my chest. I hold her close and pray we can stay like this forever, just she and I, soaking up every ounce of happiness we just created.

Chapter 11

Freya

I don't know how it happened, but I've been staying with Luca and the Three Stooges for a few days now. Okay, so I do know how it happened. Luca has me dick drunk and the dogs are too freaking cute and cuddly to leave for more than a few hours at a time. My life is perfect. And it's terrifying as shit.

Luca is making me rethink everything I've ever wanted out of life, and I'm not sure how I feel about that. I want to trust it, but what if it all falls apart? I've never been as invested in another person as I am with Luca. Aside from Leena, of course, but this is different.

Good thing she got back from her honeymoon yesterday. I need some "girl talk" as Luca likes to call it. I can't help the cheesy smile that spreads across my face when I think about the early days when I first met Luca.

Darlene was staying with Matteo for her own protection, but I made sure she promised to call me every afternoon at four. Her calls were supervised for a while by Luca. I giggle to myself, remembering how he thought he was being so stealthy. I knew from day one there was someone else in the room with her. I didn't know, however, that they would become the most important person to me. The center of my world. The only one who could crush me completely.

Mo meows loudly, diverting my attention.

"Oh yeah? You got something to say, mister?" He just looks at me expectantly, as cats often do. "You're not getting more treats. You've had plenty already."

Mo doesn't waver. Neither do I. Then he rubs his soft, furry body against my leg and purrs so sweetly. How could I not give in?

"Fine," I huff, bending down to scoop Mo up and cuddle with him on the way to the kitchen. His "treats" are really just the star-shaped pieces of kibble from the dog food. He doesn't seem to like the square pieces or the round ones. Just the stars. What a diva.

"Are you giving Mo more treats?" Luca calls from down the hall.

"Uh…"

"Let me rephrase that," he says, his voice getting closer until he's standing in the doorway to the kitchen. "Are you rewarding Mo's attention-seeking behavior?"

"And so what if I am?" I sass, pouring a few stars out of the plastic baggie we keep them in.

Luca's arms are around me in the next second, pulling my back into his front as he nuzzles my neck. "Will you reward my attention seeking behavior?" He murmurs into the shell of my ear.

"It would only be fair, I suppose."

Luca grunts and spins me around, taking my lips in a punishing kiss. I feel his tongue everywhere, tangling with my tongue, lapping at me, lightly teasing the roof of my mouth, making me shiver in his arms.

When we break apart, Luca surprises me with a hug. He tucks my head under his chin and rocks me back and forth. It's so freaking sweet and unexpected, which perfectly summarizes Luca. At least when he's with me.

"You okay?" I ask, hugging him back.

"I'm great," he mumbles into the top of my head, placing a kiss there. "I want you to know it's not just your sexy curves and addictive lips I crave. It's this." He emphasizes his point by squeezing me tighter. "I want...I want intimacy with you." Luca scoffs at his own words and pulls away from me. "Does that make me sound like a pussy?"

I grab his wrist and tug him towards me. I know I can't possibly move this man if he didn't want to go somewhere, seeing as he's nearly a foot taller than me and made of pure muscle and steel, but Luca comes willingly, folding me up into his arms again.

"I think it makes you pure and genuine," I whisper into his chest. "I think it makes you honest and sweet and perfect."

"Then why do you sound so sad?"

Do I? Am I? The same thoughts I had earlier come flooding back.

This is too good. I don't deserve this kind of attention. It won't last.

"What are you thinking about so hard, baby?"

My entire body gets a warm fuzzy feeling whenever he calls me that. I can't help it. Apparently, I like pet names. But only from Luca.

I sigh, knowing I need to be as transparent with him as he just was with me. Luca has been putting himself out there for days now, showing me who he is at his core, even if he doesn't realize it. I want to let him in too, but I always seem to choke on the words.

"This is perfect," I shrug. "Too perfect. I keep waiting for you to get tired of me, or for me to screw this up somehow. It's too good, right? We can't possibly just be...happy, can we?"

Luca contemplates my words while holding me close, right there in the middle of the kitchen. I don't know why that detail sticks out to me. I guess it shows me he'd drop anything, anywhere, to provide me the comfort I need. My eyes burn with tears, but I refuse to let them fall.

"Before I met you, I would have said no. I can't just be happy. That's not who I am or what I deserve. I'm still working on the deserving part, but there's no denying you make me the happiest motherfucker in the whole damn world. Happy doesn't cover it. You make me..."

Luca sighs and peels me off his chest, wiping away the few tears that escaped. "You make me look forward to each day, simply because I know I will learn more about you. I'll discover a new smile or a new ticklish spot." He pinches me right below my ribcage, making me jerk and giggle in his arms. "If I'm really lucky, I get to see more of how your beautiful mind works, or how you manage to be stubborn and ruthless while also being kind and thoughtful."

"Luca...I don't even know what to say," I whisper, swallowing around the lump in my throat.

"That's alright, baby girl. I've got you."

I nod and let myself melt into him, wanting to believe with everything I am this man means what he says.

Luca's phone beeps, breaking our little moment. He grunts, making me smile and roll my eyes at him. How can he give me these crazy heartfelt confessions one minute and then switch to monosyllabic grunts the next? I love that he's only sweet with me. Fuck everyone else, Luca is mine.

"Ready to head to the compound?" He asks after checking the incoming text.

I nod, getting my emotions under control until I can dump them all over Leena and have her sort them out for me. She's a married woman now, after all, which means she knows a fuck of a lot more than I do about relationships.

Ten minutes later, I'm skipping through the Moscatelli mansion to find Darlene. I already know she's in the library. Sure enough, I push through the ridiculous double doors and find my bestie curled up in a chair with her first edition copy of *Beauty and the Beast*.

I don't know if she's aware of it or not, but Leena has a hand resting on her belly, where she's growing a freaking kid. It still boggles my mind. She's not showing yet, which is why it's so endearing that her hand is resting on her stomach. I notice she's whispering the words out loud as she reads them. Is she reading to her unborn baby? Darlene is too precious.

She looks up, finally noticing me. Her big, bright smile brings such joy to my heart.

"Freya!" She practically yells, hopping off the chair and throwing her arms around me.

"Shh, don't you know this is a library?" I stage whisper. Leena laughs and grabs my hand, leading me over to the couch. "So? Tell me everything! How was Thailand?"

"Magical," she sighs dreamily. Then her cheeks turn bright red, and I'm guessing she's picturing some sights that have nothing to do with Thailand itself. My sweet, innocent little Leena has grown into quite the dirty girl. I can't blame her. I've done the same. "Tell me about you! How's Luca?"

"He's… Wait, why would you ask about him?" Jesus, am I that transparent? I've hardly spoken a few sentences to her in over a week, how does she know about Luca?

Leena just smiles, her bright blue eyes glowing with excitement. "So, is there something you want to tell me?"

"I didn't say that."

"But there is, right?"

"Fine, yes, there are lots of things to tell you. Like I have three dogs now. Larry, Curly, and Mo. Well, one is a cat who has a dog complex. I broke them out of the shelter and Luca took them in, which is how we sort of...you know."

Darlene stares at me for a beat, then gets that big cheesy grin on her face. "I'll need to meet my nephews soon, and I definitely want to hear more about the great escape, but right now I need every single detail! Have you guys…?"

She wiggles her eyebrows, which is such a Leena thing to do. It's dorky and funny as hell, while also being sweet and endearing. God, I love her so much. I missed her more than I realized. For some reason, that makes my eyes fill up with tears for the second time today.

"Freya? What's wrong? Did he hurt you? I have a gun now, you know. Matteo taught me how to use one properly. I'm sure he'll be pissed that I killed off his second in command, but he'd back me up. Plus, he knows how to get rid of the body. There are definitely perks to being married to a mafia boss."

I laugh through my tears at her outburst. Leena is still sweet and innocent in a lot of ways, but after she was kidnapped, she found her strength. She's only grown into it more over the last few months, which I love seeing. Matteo is good for her.

"I won't be requiring your services just yet," I smile at her once I've wiped away my tears. "I'm afraid, Leena. Fucking terrified." I run through the conversation Luca and I had this morning in my head, trying to recapture what I told him so I can get Leena's opinion. "It feels too good to be true, which in my experience, means it is. I don't know how to get over that. I don't know how to trust someone with all of me."

"I get it. I still feel like I'm living in a fairy tale most days. Some mornings I wake up thinking it's all a dream. Instead of asking myself what will happen if it all goes wrong, I started asking myself what will happen if everything goes right? Do I really want to throw away the best thing that has ever happened to me because I'm too scared to accept good things?"

"Easier said than done," I grumble. Leena laughs and rolls her eyes at me.

"Well then, just do it already!"

I glare at her but then laugh. "I also feel like I'm changing."

Darlene is quiet, slowly nodding her head. "Changing in a good way or a bad way?"

"I don't know. I never thought I'd be *that* girl. The one who meets some guy and suddenly wants to jump into a fantasy and gives up everything about herself to please him."

"Is that what's happening?"

"No, but—"

"Ah, ah, ah. You can't project your insecurities onto Luca. He can't be blamed for how you've been hurt in the past. That's not fair."

I glare at her again, wondering when she became so wise. I guess being married really does give you special insight into these things. Or maybe it's the fact that she knows me better than anyone else.

"*But*," I continue, "I am changing. It's a slippery slope, right?"

"Change isn't always bad, you know. Has he changed who you are at your core, or is he changing what you want out of life?"

I take a few moments to think about her question. I'm still me. Maybe even more so than before. Luca said he likes discovering new things about me, and I think I'm discovering new things about myself, too.

"I guess he's changing what I want out of life."

"That's not necessarily bad. Plans change along with your priorities. You were willing to change up your routine for Larry, Curly, and Mo, right? I'm guessing Luca is a little more important than them?"

I nod slowly, taking in her answer. She's right. Of course, she's right. What were my plans, anyway? I still don't know, but I think I'd follow Luca anywhere. That thought shoots fear and excitement into my veins.

Darlene finally breaks the silence.

"Does he make you feel ashamed for who you are? Or heck, have you even shown him who you are? I know how little you reveal of yourself to the world."

"He's seen me," I whisper. "Most of me, anyway. More than anyone else. No offense," I grin at her. Leena just smiles and nods, and I know she knows what I mean. Matteo is her person, the one who gets all of her. Could Luca really be mine? My person? "And I don't feel shame around him. I feel...like I can breathe."

When Darlene doesn't say anything for a few moments, I look over at her, surprised to see tears in her eyes.

"I'm sorry, these dang pregnancy hormones have me crying at the drop of a hat. Freya, that's beautiful. Have you told him that?"

"Not yet."

"Does he feel the same way?"

I go over all of the sweet things he said this morning. Hell, all of the sweet things he's said over the last ten days. I cherish every single one of them. I might not be able to express my emotions very well, but I've gathered up his words and hold them close to my heart; closer than anything has ever been before.

"Yeah. I really think he does."

"Then what are you waiting for?!"

"Uh…" Well, when she puts it like that, I feel like an idiot. An idiot who still has a lot of insecurities, but one who realizes she'll never get over her fears if she keeps running away from good things.

"I think now is your chance," Leena whispers before nodding her head towards the door.

Luca is trying to hide in the shadow of one of the large library doors, but he's too big to hide anywhere. It's awfully funny to watch him try, though. I wonder how much Luca heard? Does he think I'm an idiot too?

"Go on," Leena shoos me away. "And call me later. I need the deets!"

I nod at her, but I'm already headed towards Luca, my big, scary, teddy bear of a mafia man.

Luca doesn't apologize for eavesdropping, which makes me like him even more. I truly believe this man wouldn't ever lie to me or hide anything from me. Can I do the same for him?

Chapter 12

Freya

I grab Luca by his tie and drag him out of the library. He chuckles and follows where I lead. That thought settles deep inside of me, opening up doors I thought I had closed for good.

When we get into the hallway, I turn and throw my arms around him, my lips seeking his. Luca wraps me up in his embrace, lifting me off the ground as he returns my kiss with just as much pent-up need as I have for him.

He presses my back against the wall, both of us mostly hidden behind a big creepy statue of a nearly naked man. Rich people are so fucking weird.

I don't have time to dwell on that thought, seeing as Luca is grinding his massive cock against my stomach. A deliciously wicked idea pops into my head. One I can't ignore.

I slip out of Luca's arms, laughing when he growls in disapproval. His scowl doesn't last long when he sees me get down on my knees.

"Freya, what are you doing?"

"Whatever the fuck I want," I grin up at him. I untuck his shirt and claw my way into his pants before he can say anything else.

"Christ, woman. What you do to me," he hisses out as I slowly stroke him up and down.

I lean over and kiss the tip of his dick, smirking to myself when it grows in my hand and starts leaking precum. I lick up the pearly drop, then kiss down the side of his hard cock, taking my sweet time enjoying him. Well, enjoying his agony. I feel Luca practically vibrating with need. For me. That thought has me soaking my panties.

"Fucking hell, get your mouth on me right now, baby girl. Don't tease me."

I lift an eyebrow at him, staring right into his captivating blue eyes as I slowly lick up the underside of his cock, massaging the bulging nerve there with my tongue. Luca curses again and braces himself against the wall, caging me in beneath his large frame.

I take mercy on him and swallow as much of his girth as I can. He's freaking huge and I only get about halfway down before I'm choking on him. Luca doesn't seem to mind. He leans into the wall, biting his balled-up fist. I feel fucking powerful knowing the effect I have on him. Knowing he's in a vulnerable position, and he's trusting me with all of him.

"Shit, baby, gotta stop," he groans, tangling his fingers in my hair and tugging me away from his angry shaft.

I pout, but only for a second. Luca pulls me up, grips my thighs, and has me pressed against the wall with my legs around his hips before I get a chance to even take a breath. He slides my panties to the side and rams his huge fucking cock inside of me in one hard thrust. God, I'm glad I decided to wear a dress today.

Luca pins me to the wall and hammers in and out of me, fucking the air right out of my lungs. I bow my back, baring my neck to him as he kisses and bites his way towards my chest. Luca pulls the top of my dress down with his teeth, followed by the cup of my bra.

I bite my lips, trying not to cry out when he licks my nipple and then pulls it through his teeth. My hands wrap around the back of his head, holding him there while we rock into each other. Each swirl of his tongue on my sensitive nipple shoots lighting straight to my clit, making me grind down on him harder.

Each time the head of Luca's dick hits the very end of me, my nerves spark and my muscles tense, almost to the point of pain.

"I feel you, Freya. You want to come for me, don't you?" He whispers into the hollow of my throat before licking a line up to my chin and nipping my jaw.

"Y-yes…" I moan. "Yes, yes, yes…"

Luca growls and angles his hips, hitting me higher, harder, faster than before. I shake uncontrollably in his arms and wrap myself around him, clinging to his muscular frame while he pounds into me, over and over, again and again, one more time...

And then he pulls out.

I almost sob at the loss, but Luca sets me down and spins me around, forcing me to brace myself on the wall with my hands out. He grabs my hips, pulls my panties down, and thrusts inside of me, making me come instantly.

Luca's large hand covers my mouth just as a scream is ripped from deep in my chest. I gasp for air, trembling and moaning and still riding the wave of never-ending bliss.

His other hand slips around to my front, and then I feel his fingers circling my clit, sending me up and over before I even come back down from my first orgasm. Sharp, exquisite pain zaps through my body, stealing my strength as my pussy bears down on his cock, sucking him back inside when he tries pulling out.

"Fuck, fuck, fuck, little girl, you're fucking unreal, do you know that? Jesus," he grunts into the shell of my ear, his hot breath tickling my heated skin, making me gush even more for him.

"Luca, please…"

"Please, what?"

"I...I don't know, just…"

He growls and moves his hands to my breasts, squeezing them roughly and using them as leverage to tear into me, each savage thrust going deeper, deeper, so fucking deep I feel like I'm choking on him.

I can barely stand, but I somehow feel like I'm right at my peak again, climbing higher, higher, impossibly higher…

Then he pinches my nipples, *hard*. I'm thrown over the cliff into a dark pool of inky, black bliss. I feel weightless, boneless, and so, *so* fucking wet. I feel Luca's pace grow frantic as he ruts into me. Then he stills and growls into my shoulder, the sound vibrating through me as he empties rope after rope of cum into my still-convulsing pussy.

"Holy fuck," he mumbles. I laugh breathlessly and rest my forehead on the wall in front of me.

I'm about to open my mouth to say the same thing, but then the library doors swing open, and Darlene comes skipping out. She might turn left to go to her room, but she could also turn right to go downstairs. That would mean she would walk right past us. Luca and I freeze. He presses me further into the wall, trying to hide us completely behind the creepy as fuck statue.

He's still buried inside of me, amazingly still hard. I squeeze my pussy around him, making him inhale sharply. "Careful," he warns, though I feel him lengthen more and slowly grind down on me.

I don't say anything, I just press my ass into him, meeting him shallow thrust for shallow thrust.

"We gotta stop," he murmurs, still circling his hips. His cock scrapes against my G-spot, making me spasm and whimper. Luca fists my hair and yanks my head to the side, devouring my lips and swallowing down my cries.

He grunts and grinds and kisses me breathless. I tear my mouth away from him and hold my breath as my body stretches, tenses, expands...and then implodes. My cunt goes crazy, snapping around Luca's thickness again and again, uncontrollably.

Luca wraps his arms around me to hold me up as he thrusts inside of me one last time, finding his release.

I have no idea if Darlene saw us and ran away, or if she didn't notice at all, and truthfully, I can't bring myself to care. Luca buries his face into the side of my neck and lets out a breath before pulling out of me and turning me around.

He looks a little sheepish, which is so freaking cute, I have no choice but to kiss his chin. Luca cups my cheek and pulls my head up so he can kiss me properly.

"That was a close call," he whispers into my parted lips before kissing me again.

"Mmhm," I agree, diving back into his mouth. I can't help it. I think I could go again right here, right now. As soon as I can feel my legs, that is.

Luca leans back, breaking our kiss. I pout, which makes him grin. God, I could really get used to this. Having fun with Luca. Making love to Luca. Teasing Luca, building a life with Luca, loving Luca.

Holy shit. Love?

"Hey. Stay here with me. Stay right here in this moment with me," he whispers. "This is real, Freya. You and me. Just like this." I don't say anything, still too stunned by the overwhelming idea of loving Luca. "Tell me you don't feel what I'm feeling right now."

"What are you feeling?"

Luca tips my chin up and rests his forehead on mine. "I feel forever, *la mia anima*."

"I feel it, too," I whisper so quietly I don't know if he heard me.

"Thank fuck."

With that, Luca kisses me one last time before helping me get put back together. He laces his fingers through mine and pulls me down the hallway towards his office. I shove down the doubts and the big, scary, unanswerable questions and focus on what Leena said.

What if everything goes right?

Chapter 13

Luca

I still smell like sex, even after cleaning up in the bathroom. I can't bring myself to care, even though I'm stepping into a meeting with Matteo.

Jesus Christ, Freya is fucking incredible. Hallway sex? Never thought I'd be into that, but holy fuck, I am now. I'm pretty sure I'd be into anything Freya wanted to try.

It was more than just amazing sex, though. I know Freya felt it too. She's felt it all along, but today she allowed herself to acknowledge it. Us. Forever.

"Luca," Matteo greets, clearing his throat. "How're...things?" He raises an eyebrow and has a smirk on his face. The cocky bastard is aware of everything that goes on in the family. Of course he knows about Freya and me, too.

"Ah, personally or professionally?" I hedge. The answers are very different.

"Come on, Luca. You and I are more than business associates in the crime world. You're my family, my real family. Tell me about you, first."

I gawk at him but recover quickly. I should be used to this changed man in front of me. He's shown a softer side, at least to me, ever since he and Darlene got together. He's still every bit a terrifying, feared leader, but he's...human. Darlene brought that out in him. Much like Freya is doing for me.

"Well, I assume you're asking because you know about me and Freya?"

Matteo chuckles and then smiles – another new thing for him. Me too. "I've known about Freya since the day you two got in an argument over the phone about Darlene being kidnapped." Matteo's features grow dark, likely at the memory of that horrible day. "Despite being worried out of my fucking mind, I knew she got under your skin."

I just nod, taking time to contemplate my response. "Right. So, yeah. We're, uh, together."

"Together? As in...?"

"What do you mean?"

"What do *you* mean? What is she to you? Are you just sleeping with her? Is it more serious than that? Is she your girlfriend?"

"Woah, why does this feel like a father interrogating his daughter's boyfriend on the first date?"

Matteo shrugs. "She doesn't have a father who's going to do that for her."

"Fair enough," I sigh. "I'm not just sleeping with her. Freya is...complicated. Frustrating. Challenging. But she's...I think she's everything." I rub the back of my neck and look away from him. We've never had a heart to heart like this. I've not only felt things I've never felt before this week, but I seem to be telling everyone about my feelings as well. It can take a toll on a guy.

Matteo seems to pick up on how uncomfortable I am and mercifully changes the subject. But not before giving me one last piece of advice.

"I get it. I'm glad you've found each other. Be good to her, Luca."

"Always." We share a look. One that tells him I'm dead fucking serious about taking care of my woman.

"Great. Now that we've had 'the talk' Darlene wanted me to give you, let's get down to business."

I have to chuckle at that. Of course, it was Darlene's idea. She had her talk with Freya, so Matteo is here giving me a talking to of my own. I felt a little bad about eavesdropping on the girls, but not enough to walk away when I realized they were talking about me. I didn't hear everything, but I heard enough.

Freya said I make her feel like she can breathe. Fuck if that didn't nearly bring me to my knees. I know how hard it was for her to say that out loud. I just pray one day she'll trust me enough to tell me face to face.

Matteo clears his throat, though he's smirking again like he knew I was lost in thought about my woman. Bastard.

"Okay. Right," I sigh, switching gears. "Ernesto Mazzi, the new Don of the Ricci family, is a fucking lowlife. Scum of the earth."

"That's to be expected in our line of business, I suppose. Did you figure out how the hell he became head of the Ricci's after Stefano got a bullet in his ugly mug?"

"Yeah. Turns out Nicky isn't Stefano's only kid. He had a daughter, too."

"What the fuck? How did we not know about this?"

"Apparently, Stefano pretty much kept her locked away her whole life."

"A princess in a tower, huh?"

"Yeah. He was saving her to form an alliance. Stefano promised his daughter's, uh, innocence and hand in marriage to Ernesto some time last year. The marriage was already set to take place when she turned eighteen."

"She's not even eighteen yet? Jesus. What's the girl's name?"

"Alessia Ricci. Her eighteenth birthday was last week, but the wedding hasn't happened yet."

Matteo nods his head and rubs his temples. "Okay," he finally says, taking a deep breath. "So, Ernesto is basically taking over because of his future marriage to Alessia; he views it as a right to the throne, so to speak. How does Nicky feel about being second in command? Is there potential to get him to turn?"

"Doubt it, but it could be worth a shot. He's been silent on the subject, at least whenever he meets with Ernesto at the Ricci family restaurant. We were only able to get so many bugs distributed without being caught."

"And what advantage would Stefano have received from giving his daughter away to Ernesto? He's not part of another family that could potentially form an alliance or anything. He seems like a nobody who somehow clawed his way to the top out of nowhere."

"Still working on that part. Whatever it is must be big. Big enough to take them down."

Again, Matteo nods, though this time he gets up from the seat behind his desk and starts pacing.

"What if we got the girl?"

"What do you mean?"

"Alessia. What if we brought her here and got her to talk?"

"You want to torture Stefano's daughter?"

"Fuck, no. I want her to turn on her family. Surely she doesn't want to be given away to an old fuck like Ernesto."

"Yeah, especially considering he's been married four times and each of his wives mysteriously disappeared."

"Shit. Well, exactly, then. Sounds like Alessia has been treated poorly her whole life. We offer her freedom and protection in exchange for useful information."

"Makes sense."

"Figure out a way to get a message to her. Make it vague enough that if she's caught, it won't lead back to us, but still let her know what we're offering and give her a way to signal her approval."

"Right. Not enough information, yet specific information. No problem," I grumble.

Matteo claps me on the shoulder and chuckles. "I have faith in you, Luca. Now get out of here. We both have other people we need to see right now, don't we?"

I picture Freya's mischievous little grin and sparkling green eyes. "Yeah, there's someone else I'd like to see," I agree.

We shake hands and part ways, both of us on the hunt for our women.

***

I was caught on the way out of the compound by a few of the guys who needed to discuss something they overheard about Nicky Ricci. I'm glad Matteo was also there because I honestly have no idea what they said. The whole time I was thinking about Freya and how much I miss her, which is fucking insane. I saw her this morning. But there's no denying the ache in my chest when I think about holding her.

I finally walk in the front door to my house and am greeted with the most beautiful sight. Freya is standing in the kitchen wearing a sexy, vintage blue dress that flares out at the hips. Her bright red hair is twisted up into a bun on the top of her head, revealing her slender neck. The look is complete with a light pink apron with lace trim.

I notice her feet are bare, and something about that tugs at my heart. She's comfortable in my space. Freya looks completely at ease right here in my kitchen and fuck, do I want to keep her there forever. Not in my kitchen, per se, but in my home. Our home.

Suddenly, Freya spins around on her heel, giving me a cute little scowl, along with a sexy ass grin.

"Don't get used to me making you dinner every night," she says, pointing a wooden spoon at me and flinging whatever sauce she was just stirring all around the kitchen.

That's when it hits me.

I fucking love her. I love the wild, chaotic, messy, loud, disaster of a woman with a heart of gold buried under layers of sarcasm and sass.

All of the air leaves my lungs as my mind scrambles to wrap around this new fact. I don't know how I didn't see it before now. I mean, I've talked of forever with her, but I didn't dare hope I was capable of actually loving someone.

Watching her now, as her scowl turns into a playful smile, I know it's true. This overwhelming feeling of protectiveness, thankfulness, safety, and warmth has to be love. It's tinged with vulnerability and the knowledge that losing her would destroy me, but it's worth it. The fear is worth the joy and pleasure I can give Freya.

"I know, I know, you're probably speechless at my domesticity, but like I said, this isn't going to be a regular occurrence. I just had a craving for gnocchi and salsa di pomodoro, and my recipe is better than anyone else's. No offense to all the Italian restaurants you guys have in your pocket." Freya winks at me, letting me know she's not sorry at all.

I clear my throat, trying like hell to recover so I can actually hold a conversation with the woman who captivates me – mind, body, and soul.

"You know how to make gnocchi?" It's a dumb thing to say, I realize, but the question pops out before I can stop it.

Freya turns around to tend to the stove and shrugs. "Yeah, yeah, I look as Irish as it gets, but that doesn't mean I can't cook a mean Italian dish."

I grin and make my way into the kitchen, wrapping my arms around her waist and pulling her back into my front.

"What else can you cook, *la mia anima*?" I ask, placing a soft kiss on the side of her neck. My chest grows tight when she sighs and relaxes ever so much. I fucking love that my touch, my kiss, my presence relaxes her.

"Okay, so this might be the *only* Italian dish I can make, or any dish, really, but it's still the best." I chuckle at her answer and kiss her neck again. "My stepmom taught me when I was little. She grew up in Italy," Freya adds softly, like the words hurt to get out. "She died when I was nine."

I press my lips to her temple and breathe in her lavender and saltwater scent. There are still so many things I don't know about her, but these little crumbs she gives me are enough for now. I know how difficult each confession is for her, so I treasure her words, her heart, her sadness, and sorrow.

"I'm sorry you lost her so early on. I can tell she was special to you."

Freya nods and then leans her head against my shoulder while we sway back and forth. I don't know what it is about that – holding her and rocking her in my arms, but it soothes me. I'm pleased to know it soothes her, too.

The moment becomes too much for her. Freya leans forward and wiggles out of my embrace.

"Go sit down, it's almost done. You can thank me for slaving over a hot stove all day when we're done eating."

"Dammit, woman," I groan, knowing I'm going to be distracted with all the ways I want to thank her, and not just for the meal, either.

A few minutes later, Freya sets a plate full of gnocchi slathered in salsa di pomodoro in front of me. A salad appears next to it, and then a glass of wine. The perfect meal.

Freya talks about her visit with Darlene, the Three Stooges, and a potential part-time job as a barista. I can't do anything but watch her. The way her full, soft lips form words, how her nose scrunches up adorably when she tells me about a client she's working with who is being difficult, how her emerald eyes sparkle playfully when Mo starts begging for food like the dog he thinks he is.

It's perfect. She's perfect. I love her. I fucking love every single thing about her, even when she's pushing all of my goddamn buttons.

I'm jarred out of my thoughts by the sound of a chair scraping across the floor. Freya is standing up with an angry look on her beautiful face. Shit.

"I definitely won't cook for you if you're not even going to eat it," she grumbles before reaching for my plate.

I look down and realize I haven't even taken a bite. Fuck. I'm already screwing this up.

I grab the plates out of her hand, setting them on the table before I loop my fingers around her wrist and pull Freya down into my lap. She fights me at first, but I know she doesn't really want to leave. She wants someone worth staying for. I want to be that person for her.

"I'm sorry, baby girl. It's not you, it's—"

"Really?! *It's not you, it's me*? Are you kidding me right now?"

"Freya, no, that's not what I was going to say."

"Whatever, if you're going to break up with me, just do it already. Waste of gnocchi," she mutters.

This woman. Nothing will ever come easy, but I don't mind. I'll fight for her with every breath in my body.

I cup the side of her face with one hand and tighten my hold on her hip, keeping her anchored in my lap. "Listen to me, Freya. I'm sorry I've been distracted tonight. The thing is...I walked in the door and saw you standing in the kitchen looking adorable and sexy as fuck and I realized I loved you more than I thought possible."

"Oh," she whispers so softly I almost don't hear her. Freya's sharp green eyes search mine, and I watch as my words sink into her heart. Her eyes water, but before the first tear can fall, she buries her face into the side of my neck. I wrap my arms around her while silent tears wet my skin.

I can feel her trembling as she clings to me, to my declaration of love. I don't expect her to say it back. That's not why I told her. I just needed Freya to know where I stand. I mean, fuck, she thought I was going to break up with her. That's never going to happen.

"I love you, too," she murmurs. "I'm terrified of how much I love you, Luca. Please don't hurt me."

"Never. Never, *la mia anima*. Do you know what that means?" She shakes her head no, and I peel her off my chest so I can look at her when I say this. I need to know she understands the depths of my feelings for her. "It means *my soul*. That's what you are. I was wandering around the earth without my soul. Until you came into my life. Now you're mine. My soul."

Freya gasps softly, and then leans forward, kissing me with everything she has. I taste the salt of her tears mixed with the natural sweetness of her lips. I cup the back of her neck and tilt her head so I can dive deeper, taste more of her, give her everything in return.

When we break apart, I rest my forehead on hers, savoring this moment. It will be branded on my heart for all eternity.

Freya leans back and gives me a mischievous grin. "So now that we've got that all cleared up, can I warm up your dinner?"

I throw my head back and laugh, something I can't seem to stop doing when I'm around her. Freya kisses my chin and hops off my lap, taking my plate over to the microwave. I can't believe she's mine. I can't believe she loves me, too.

Chapter 14

Freya

Luca loves me.

He loves me almost as much as I love him. Maybe even more, which is crazy. I want to stand on top of Willis Tower and shout about how Luca and I found each other. It's cliché and sappy as fuck, but true. I want everyone to know Luca somehow finds *me* worthy to love.

We spent most of last night proving to each other exactly how crazy in love we are, which is why I'm dead on my feet today. Six orgasms in one night with the sexist beast of a man I've ever seen? Totally worth it.

Luca got up early and went to the compound to deal with whatever mafia drama is going on at the moment. I slept in and played with the dogs, and now I'm on my way to see Leena. We haven't had much of a chance to talk since she encouraged me to think about everything going right with Luca instead of everything going wrong.

That girl. Sexy, sweet, and wise. Matteo is one lucky son of a bitch, that's for sure. He knows it too, which is why I allowed them to be together in the first place. I grin to myself and shake my head as I walk to the library to find my bestie. I know I couldn't keep them apart, but I sure could make Matteo's life a lot more annoying if I wanted to. Good thing he dotes on Leena and treats her like the queen she is.

On my way to the library, I decide to take a quick detour to see Luca. I can't help it. I seem to crave his touch, and not just in a sexual way. I want his hand on the small of my back, or for him to tuck my hair behind my ear.

It's all of those little gestures that really do me in. The calming presence he always emanates is magnified when he touches me. I've always had nervous, fidgety habits and excess energy, but Luca makes it easier for me to relax. Easier to breathe, just like I told Darlene.

What's more is those sweet touches seem to come so naturally to Luca, despite him growing up without any love and not wanting human contact. Until me, that is. I love that I brought that out in him. It's one more reason to trust him – knowing he trusts *me* enough to let me in and let me love him that way.

I never really understood the saying "butterflies in my stomach" when someone went gaga over some dude. But right now, I swear I have about a billion manic butterflies swarming around, tickling my insides as I make my way towards Luca's office.

I'm almost at my destination when I hear angry voices coming from Matteo's office, right next to Luca's.

And then I hear the name of the man who has haunted my dreams for the last five years.

"Ernesto fucking Mazzi!" Matteo roars. "He knew about the bugs. He purposefully fed us a lie to throw us off track."

Those butterflies from earlier turn to stone and sink into the pit of my stomach. I've thought of that night over and over throughout the years. I knew, I fucking *knew* I wasn't safe. I've never been safe. I'll never be safe.

I clap my hand over my mouth to hold in my sob. I press myself against the wall next to the closed door and listen for the rest. I need to know how fucked I am.

"How many fucking moles do we have?" Matteo yells again. I can hear his heavy footsteps as he paces back and forth. "I've been too lenient."

"Too distracted is more like it," someone mutters.

"What the fuck did you say, Thomas?" Matteo's voice is quieter now, yet somehow more threatening.

"I'm just saying. I'm glad you found your girl. You too, Luca. But..."

"But?" Luca grits out.

"You've both been distracted is all."

A heavy silence blankets the room. Finally, Matteo sighs. "I will never regret finding and loving my angel. She will always come first. *Always*." He pauses for a moment before continuing. "But I see your point. It's time to clean house, boys. Starting at the top."

I try to control my breathing, but I can't seem to pull enough air into my lungs. I slump against the wall before my trembling legs give out and send me crashing to the floor. I'm both sweaty and freezing at the same time, my body temperature apparently as out of control as the rest of me. The familiar sting of my nails digging into my palms brings me back from the edge.

"You launching an investigation against us?" Someone else asks.

"Do I need to?"

"No, boss," he's quick to answer. "You know how loyal I am. The things I've done for the family."

Matteo grunts before saying, "I know, Rocco. The men in this room are the only ones I trust. Everyone else is a suspect and will be investigated and monitored. You five are to start with the captains. Make them prove their loyalty by any means you see fit. Once they pass, move down the ranks until we've flushed the rats out. I'll send them back to Ernesto in a body bag."

Shit. Shit, shit, shit. This is bad. I *knew* the other shoe was going to drop, I just didn't expect it to be like this. I thought Luca would break my heart, not the other way around.

Another person clears their throat, almost tentatively, if that's a thing. "At the risk of getting my ass kicked, I feel like I need to point out the two newest members of the family."

There's a long, tension-filled pause that I can *feel* from my hiding spot in the hallway. Matteo breaks the silence with a deadly tone.

"I know you aren't suggesting that Darlene is a fucking mole for the Ricci family. Tell me, Emilio. Tell me you're not stupid enough to think something like that, let alone say it out loud."

"Look, you know my loyalty, you know I always put the family first. I'm just making sure our bases are covered, boss. You said you wanted to start at the top…"

"Darlene is not the mole. End of story."

I know what's coming before he even says it.

"What about Freya?"

Luca roars, making me jump and accidentally knock my shoulder into yet another creepy as hell stone statue. Seriously, how many of these things does Matteo have?

I manage to catch the statue before it crashes to the ground. I can't hear any more. I need to get away. If they launch a full investigation, they'll find exactly what they're looking for. Ties to Ernesto? Check. Hacker skills I stupidly paraded around? Check. An attempt to scrub my time in juvie off my record? Check.

I stumble back down the hallway on shaky legs, somehow managing to get out to my car without either throwing up or collapsing. My hands are trembling so bad it takes me several attempts to get my key in the ignition. I ignore the pounding headache and painful thud of my heart and pull away from the Moscatelli compound for the last time. It's that thought that sends me over the edge.

I pull over on the side of the road once I'm several blocks away, and let the tears fall. Violent sobs shudder through my body and rattle my bones, but I can't stop. I was so stupid to think I could hide from Ernesto. One way or another, this was all going to come back and bite me in the ass. I just pray that Luca will be spared if I leave. It hurts so fucking much to think that my past could ruin Luca's future and his standing in the family.

Fuck. They aren't going to kick him out, they're going to fucking kill him if they suspect I'm the mole and he's been working with me. I have to leave. It's for his own good. Darlene's too, though I know Matteo wouldn't let anything happen to her. Still, they can't be associated with me.

Is it already too late? Did I just put the only man I've ever loved in danger? I don't know. I don't fucking know what to do, but I can't stay here.

I wipe the last of my tears away and take a deep breath. I've prepared for this moment. I have everything in place to bail out of my life here in Chicago; I just never thought I'd actually do it.

Thirty minutes later, I'm pulling into the parking lot of my building. I stopped by Luca's and said goodbye to the dogs, which officially broke my fucking heart. I also grabbed my laptop, hard drive, and a few other essentials, before wiping everything off my desktop computer. I don't have time to dispose of it properly, but at least all the information should be gone.

Inside my apartment, I grab the large duffel bag stuffed with cash, a burner phone, a fake ID, and an assortment of other necessities. I throw clothes into the bag haphazardly, pausing briefly when I see Luca's t-shirt I wore home after our first night together.

I hold it up to my nose and breathe in deeply. His scent clings to the fabric, making me tear up all over again. But I don't have time to break down, so I swallow around the tangled lump of emotion in my throat and toss the shirt in my bag as well. I already know I'm going to be a creeper about it and keep the shirt under my pillow so I can take it out and smell him at night.

After packing clothes, shoes, and toiletries, I take my laptop out and book the next flight to New York, purchasing the ticket under a shell account so whoever is looking for me will have a harder time tracking me down.

I know the mafia has more resources and connections than I can imagine, and they are capable of hacking into all my accounts, but I'm hoping it will stall them long enough for me to disappear into the Big Apple.

My phone dings with a text and I nearly jump out of my skin. It's Leena asking where I am. Shit. I type back a bullshit excuse about being sick and dodge her suggestions of bringing me soup or having a Golden Girls marathon. Fuck. I'm going to miss her so goddamn much. But I'll have time to cry about it later. Right now, I have to catch a flight.

I contemplate taking some of my kitschy, cheesy thrift store figurines, but I can't bring myself to do it. It's going to be hard enough to have Luca's shirt as a reminder of my life here.

I allow myself one minute to look around the little home I've made for myself these last three years. I'm hit with anger like I've never felt before, which is saying something. I'm fucking seething at my dead dad for getting involved with the Ricci family. For getting *me* involved with the Ricci family. I hate him. I hate that goddamn sleazy motherfucker Ernesto, too. I hate the universe for giving me a few weeks of bliss with Luca only to rip us apart by forces neither one of us can control.

"Get it the fuck together, woman," I tell myself. I straighten my back, square my shoulders, and hold my head up high. I may be garbage who came from garbage, but I can do this one noble thing. I can try to save Darlene and Luca by disappearing.

Chapter 15

Luca

"Are you fucking kidding me?" I shout, lunging at Emilio. Matteo grips my arm and squeezes tightly. It's hard to say which one of us would win in a fistfight, but I'm not about to punch the boss in the face. I have more respect for him than that.

"She sent Darlene in here with a tracking chip!" Emilio shouts back.

"Yeah, that she then used to lead us to Darlene. Fifteen Ricci men died that day, including the fucking boss! Doesn't sound like someone whose loyalties lie with the Ricci's."

"Maybe she had a change of heart last minute. She couldn't let Darlene die, so she gave you a way to find her. What you did with that information was out of her control," he shrugs as if his explanation makes perfect sense.

Fucking Emilio. Never liked the little shit. Not sure why Matteo trusts him, but it's not my place to question it. I look over at Matteo, expecting him to jump in, but he doesn't. What the fuck is happening?

"We have proof that Freya and Darlene grew up together. Their friendship is real. There's no fucking way Freya set up the whole confrontation down by the docks that led to Darlene staying here, only to have her kidnapped by the Ricci's. That makes no sense."

"What harm could it do?" Emilio asks, changing tactics. "If she's as innocent as you say she is, then why not do a little digging?" He tries to reason.

"You motherfuck—"

"Enough!" Matteo commands. "Emilio, I understand your concern. I'll handle it."

"Handle it?" I ask incredulously, wrenching my arm out of his firm grasp. "You mean you're going to stomp-kick his ass for suggesting Freya is a traitor? He accused Darlene too, or did you forget that?"

His jaw tenses as he stares Emilio down.

"Boss?" I speak again, not sure what's taking him so long to come to Freya's defense. His dark, intense eyes are focused on the ceiling, and I can tell he's lost in thought. "*Matteo*?" I grit out.

"You all have your assignments. Report back with a list of trusted captains and those we need to get rid of." With a curt nod, Matteo dismisses us.

I don't know whether to run and find Freya or stay here and potentially say something that would ruin my friendship with Matteo, not to mention my career and safety. I decide to go find Freya.

"Luca," his voice booms, letting me know I won't be going anywhere. Fine. If it's a fight he wants, bring it on.

"I can't fucking believe you," I mutter, pacing the floor after slamming the door shut.

"Listen—"

"No, you fucking listen!" I snap. I'm well aware I'm on thin ice here. Matteo and I are family – family beyond *the family*, which is the only reason he's allowing me to talk to him like this. "It's not her. How could you even think that?"

"Luca—"

"I mean, Jesus Christ, she's your wife's best friend! How—"

"*Luca!*" Matteo roars. I fall silent. Rarely does he get this worked up. "I dug into Darlene's past when she first came here. I went to her apartment and sifted through her mail, her closet, her fucking garbage can. I'm not asking you to do anything I didn't do when I was in a similar situation."

I bite back my automatic response that Freya is different from Darlene. Matteo's wife had nothing to hide, whereas my future wife has lots of secrets. I know being a spy for the Ricci's isn't one of them, however. The rest I hope to figure out in time, but only when she decides to trust me.

"You know I have to do this," Matteo continues, his voice quieter now, letting me know he's talking to me as a friend, not as the boss. "On a personal level, I get it. I understand that digging into Freya's past and monitoring her life feels like a violation of trust."

"It *is* a violation of trust," I grumble.

"However," Matteo continues, ignoring my snide remark. "I can't ignore the fact that Freya is here more often than she's not. Between having free reign of the mansion, being best friends with the queen of the Moscatelli family, and now being claimed by my second in command, Freya has access to more information than most. That's as inner circle as you get, and yet, she hasn't been vetted."

137

"But she's not—"

Matteo holds up a hand, letting me know he's not done yet. I seethe and grit my teeth, but I let him finish whatever he has to say.

"Clearing Freya's name will not only prove her loyalty, but it will show that no one comes into the family without my approval. Emilio and the other men who were in here today already have a seed of doubt planted. If I don't put Freya through the same scrutiny as everyone else, they'll always wonder. They'll start to doubt me, and once they don't trust and respect me, the whole thing comes crumbling down."

"Fine. Fuck them, then. If they don't already trust you, fucking give them the boot and find new men who don't question their leader."

Matteo sighs and scrapes a hand down his face before plopping down in his desk chair. I'm too amped up to sit, so I start pacing and clenching and unclenching my fists.

"That's not how it works, and you know it. It takes time for soldiers to move through the ranks. I can't just bring people into the inner circle, nor can I send the men I already have in the inner circle away. You know this. Once you get this close to the top, you're in for life. The only way these men are leaving is in a body bag." I open my mouth to respond, but he cuts me off again, reading my mind. "And no, I won't be getting any body bags ready. Yet."

"Fucking Christ," I mutter to myself, turning away from Matteo so I can get my shit together. I respect him, and hell, love him like a brother, though I couldn't admit that until recently. But right here, right now, I fucking hate him.

"Luca," he says, softly this time, throwing me off guard. I turn and see him with his head in his hands, looking tired and conflicted. "We both know she's hiding things. She's Darlene's best friend, and I'm not going to take her best friend away from her. Nor am I going to take your woman away from you. If we want to protect Freya, both from doubts within the walls of this compound as well as whatever outside forces we both know she's afraid of, then we have to know what we're dealing with."

I blow out a breath and try to understand where he's coming from. "So why not just ask her?"

"You know that won't be enough. We'll still need to verify everything she says, and I think we both know Freya is not going to be forthcoming with information, especially if she knows we want it so badly."

I nod my head. He's right. She wouldn't be cooperative, and fuck do I love that about her. She'd go toe to toe with the mafia. She already did in order to get Darlene back. Freya is incredible. And Matteo is right – the love of my life is in danger, not just from whatever the hell scared her that first night she stayed with me, but now from men right here inside the family.

"Fine. But once the information is collected, you and I are the only ones who will read her dossier before it's destroyed." I know I can't command Matteo to do anything, and I shouldn't be bargaining with him. But the real Matteo, the one beneath the mask of a syndicated crime lord, is a good man who knows he's pushed me to my limit.

Matteo stares me down, though not in a menacing way. He's assessing me. I let him. I have nothing to hide and he fucking knows it. Finally, he nods. "I'll make the necessary calls. We should have the information within a few hours."

"Great," I deadpan before walking towards the door. "I'm going to see Freya."

"No."

It's a simple and absolute command. My entire body tenses as I turn around. "*No?*"

"If you're seen talking to her or leaving the compound with her, our investigation will be compromised. Emilio could see you two together and it would invalidate any evidence we find that clears Freya's name. Just wait a few hours. We'll look over the dossier, then you go home to your girl knowing she's safe and has our protection."

Fuck. He's right. I know he's right. But that doesn't make it hurt any less. I ache for her. I feel like I'm betraying the only woman I've ever loved, and the only thing I want in the whole goddamn world is to hold her and apologize and promise her that I'll love her no matter what we find.

"Are you going to babysit me the whole time, or do you trust me enough to let me do my fucking job until we get the information?"

Matteo's stare turns hard, letting me know I'm close to crossing a line with him. But then his face softens, just a little. I know this is hard on him, too. Some tiny part of my brain is aware enough to realize he's been put in an impossible position, and he's trying to navigate it the best he knows how. But the rest of me is all keyed up and ready for a fight.

"Go get your work done," he finally says. "Stay close. I'll call you when I have the information."

I grunt and walk out, slamming the door for good measure. It's not nearly as satisfying as punching Emilio for starting this shit, but it'll have to do for now.

✳✳✳

Three excruciating hours later, Matteo calls me back into his office. Good thing, too, because I've been crawling out of my fucking skin with the need to get this over with and go check on Freya. The one consolation is that I know she's hanging out with Darlene, which has made it both easier and harder to keep my distance.

Knowing she's so close kills me and makes my hands twitch to feel her, touch her, hold her, and reassure her everything's going to be fine. But she's safe with Darlene, hopefully having fun and blissfully unaware of the things taking place in Matteo's office.

My heart sinks to the floor when I step inside the office. I already know whatever Matteo is scrolling through on his screen only implicates Freya further. I sit in front of Matteo's desk, waiting for him to tell me whatever the fuck has him barely containing his anger. Finally, he tears his eyes away from his computer and takes a deep breath.

"Ernesto is her uncle."

"What? That's impossible. Why would she go into foster care if she had an uncle? Plus, Freya Murphy is as Irish as it gets. No way she's related to Ernesto Mazzi. I don't buy it."

"Ernesto had a sister, Isabella Mazzi who was married to Freya's dad, Scott Murphy."

"Isabella must be her stepmom," I say, remembering what Freya told me last night while making gnocchi. "Ernesto is her step-uncle or whatever."

"Does it matter?"

I open my mouth, but the argument dies on my tongue. No, it doesn't matter. Not with something this huge. This new knowledge about Freya's family is a lot to take in. Is Ernesto the one she's been afraid of this whole time? I wish I knew. I wish she told me. All of this could have been prevented if we knew from the beginning.

Not that I'm blaming her. I don't know the whole story, but I know she wouldn't betray me or Darlene, or hell, Matteo. But this is bad.

"There's more."

"Of course there is," I mutter, bracing myself for what's next.

"Her dad owed a huge debt to the Ricci family. I'm guessing Ernesto was still rising through the ranks at the time and had connections that enabled his brother-in-law to get shady loans for whatever he was doing."

"And? He's dead now, so what does it matter?"

"Luca. You know why it matters. It's motive. Or at least, it could be seen as a motive. Spying for the Ricci's to pay off the debt. Plus, we've both experienced her hacker skills firsthand. The other men know about it, too.

"It also fits in with Emilio's theory of Freya having a change of heart and rescuing Darlene. We both know she's got a tender heart, at least for the people she cares about. There's no way Freya would let any harm come to Darlene as payment for her father's debt. And maybe…" he sighs heavily, and I know the next words out of his mouth are going to piss me the fuck off. "Maybe getting Stefano killed was part of the plan. It opened the door for Ernesto to step in."

I stand up, knocking my chair to the ground. "Un-*fucking*-believable!" I roar, pounding my fists on the desk. "Matteo, you *know* it's not her," I argue, leaning over the desk and getting in his personal space. "Fucking look at me. Look me in the eyes and tell me you think Freya is capable of that level of betrayal."

He doesn't at first. I've never been more tempted to strangle someone in my whole life, but I refrain. That's not going to get me to Freya any faster.

Matteo lifts his gaze to meet mine. I'm surprised to see hurt swimming around in his eyes, but not from betrayal. He's truly hurt at the thought of Freya being caught up in this. He's not entirely convinced of her innocence, but he knows there's more to the story.

"I don't think she did it willingly," he finally says.

"But you think she's the one leaking secrets?"

"I don't know," he sighs defeatedly. "You have to admit this all looks bad."

I step away from his desk and run my fingers through my hair, tugging at the strands. "I have to talk to her."

"I'm coming with you."

"No."

Matteo stands up and steps next to me. "I. *Am*. Coming. With. You," he states. I know there's no arguing with him.

We make our way to the library, where the girls usually end up hanging out, but when we get there, Darlene is sitting alone on the couch in front of the fireplace.

"Where's Freya?" I bark out. I know my tone is harsher than necessary, but I can't fucking help it.

"Watch it," Matteo growls.

"She's not feeling well. She canceled on me," Darlene answers, looking confused.

"You haven't seen her today?" Matteo asks, walking over to his wife and sitting down next to her, pulling her feet onto his lap.

"No. Is everything okay?"

"Everything will be fine. Don't worry, *mio tesoro*."

The two of them talk, but their voices fade into the background. All I can think about is Freya being ill. I check my phone but don't see any texts or calls from her. I send her a text asking if she's okay. Frustration boils in my veins when she doesn't immediately text me back, even though I know it's an irrational response. Then again, everything about today has been one big irrational response.

"Luca," Matteo's sharp tone pierces through my foggy thoughts. "Get over here and look at this."

He turns his phone towards me. Matteo pulled up the security feed he has sent to his phone every hour. Three hours ago, Freya's car pulled up to the compound. Five minutes later, the car speeds away.

"What does that mean?" Darlene asks in a panic. "Is she okay? What's going on?"

"I'm going after her. You can't stop me," I address Matteo.

He doesn't argue this time. "I'll do what I can from my end to ward off suspicion." I nod and nearly sprint out of the library. "Luca!" Matteo calls. "I don't know how much time I can give you. Find her, get the truth, and we can put this behind us. War is coming. We need to be focused on the real enemy."

I nod again and head out. I hear Darlene ask what he means, but I don't stick around for the conversation. Hopefully, Darlene can knock some sense into him. I'm grateful he understands why I need to leave, but I know he still has his doubts. The footage of her sneaking away sure didn't do anything to ease his suspicions.

I race to my house, *our* house, but it's empty. I suspected as much, but I still hoped she'd be sitting on the couch with the Three Stooges curled up around her.

Next, I hit up her apartment. One look in the parking lot tells me her car isn't here, but I stroll up to her door and knock anyway. No answer. I pound again, thinking maybe Freya was telling Darlene the truth and she's sleeping off a migraine or a stomachache.

When she still doesn't answer, I clench my fists, take a deep breath, and stomp-kick the rusty old hinges barely holding the plywood door together. The flimsy wood splinters. With a few more kicks, I manage to get the door loose enough to pry it open.

It says a hell of a lot about the security around here that no one even seemed to notice I was breaking down her door in the middle of the fucking day. I should feel like a deranged asshole for busting into Freya's apartment like this, but I have more important things on my mind.

"Freya!" I yell into the tiny space. It's obvious she's not here, but I check the bathroom, behind the shower curtain, under the bed, even under the fucking kitchen sink. She's gone. I know it. Not just gone from her apartment, but from me. She left me. She fucking left me.

I sink to my knees and hold my head in my hands. I'm not angry at her. I'm worried out of my goddamn mind. It hurts. It hurts so fucking bad. My soul is out there, fighting the world on her own, for reasons I don't yet understand. But I will.

I'll find her. I'll make her trust me, make her love me, make her see there's nothing too big or too scary for us to handle together. With my dying breath, I will fight to protect Freya and bring her back where she belongs, in my arms for the rest of our fucking lives.

Chapter 16

Freya

Everything hurts.

My eyes are swollen, and my head is pounding from staying up most of the night crying. Again. My back and neck ache from sleeping on a dirty, lumpy mattress that's probably been around since this rent-by-the-week motel opened in the seventies. My feet are sore from walking around the streets of New York day after day in search of a job and an apartment.

But more than that, I'm fucking shattered on the inside. Every breath hurts as it scrapes against the sharp, broken edges of my soul. Luca's soul. We're the same, and I broke us.

It's been seven days since I left, but it feels like years. I miss Luca and Darlene and the Three Stooges more than I thought possible, and I honestly don't know how I'm going to live without them. The only consolation I have is that Darlene is safe and happy with Matteo and Luca has the dogs to keep him company.

I don't even have a way to contact either one of them since I ditched my phone on the way to the airport. I smashed the SIM card and tossed the thing out the window while cruising down the highway. The Uber driver was not happy, but I don't give a fuck. I'm sure he'd understand if I explained I was running from not one, but *two* mafia families.

It's for the best, though. I have to keep reminding myself of that. I'm sure Luca and Darlene will miss me for a while, but they have to move on at some point. Larry, Curly, and Mo will forget about me after a few months, and as much as that hurts, again, it's for the best. I, on the other hand, will always be empty. They each have a piece of my heart.

"Get your ass out of bed," I grumble to myself. "No use wallowing in self-pity."

I sigh and crawl out of bed, feeling several joints pop and crack as I stretch. This fucking bed. It's about a half-step up from when I slept on the streets. Probably just as dirty, though. I shudder at the thought of who has slept – or done God knows what – here before me. Time for a shower, then I can leave this dump for a few hours.

On the bright side, the time it takes me to get ready in the morning has gone way down since the hot water only lasts about six minutes in this place. Twenty minutes later, I'm ready to go.

I pack up my computer, hoping to finish up the current project I'm working on while at the coffee shop this morning. I'm still taking hacker jobs, but I want to find something part-time as well like I did back home.

Home. I swallow back tears when I think about home. I don't picture my studio apartment, though. I picture Luca's home. I picture cuddling with the dogs in the evening until Luca comes home and joins us. I picture falling asleep in his arms and waking up to one of his rare but breathtaking smiles. I've been homeless before, but I've never felt a loss as profound as this.

I'm discovering that home isn't a place, it's a feeling I'll never get back.

"Stop it," I chastise myself. God, I need to get a part-time job so I have actual people to talk to instead of myself.

Gathering up the last of my things, I decide to stop by a cute antique store I walked by the other day in hopes they are hiring. If not, I can still look around, maybe even treat myself to a weird lamp or eclectic ceramic statue.

When I get to the store, it's surprisingly busy for a Thursday morning. Then again, everyplace around here is always busier than I think it will be. I thought Chicago was crowded, but it's got nothing on New York.

I wander around the shop, waiting for the crowd to thin out a bit before finding the manager to ask about a job. I've worked retail before, and I know there's nothing more annoying than a customer asking questions when you're clearly in the middle of a rush.

I find a section near the back of the store with funky paintings and prints from the sixties, and get lost for a bit in the bright, psychedelic colors and block screen prints of famous people. I reach for a smaller, framed print to check the price when my skin prickles with awareness. It feels like someone is watching me.

Slowly, I look to my left, pretending to be interested in a different print. Movement catches my eye like someone ducked out of the way. My breath stutters as my heart pounds painfully in my chest. I curl my hand into a fist and dig my nails into the flesh of my palm, willing the panic attack away.

It can't be. How did they find me so fast? And which family found me? It doesn't matter. I need to get the fuck out of here. Why did I choose to walk all the way to the back corner of the store? Shit. I'm trapped in here. If there really is someone watching me, he's definitely not alone.

I don't let on that I know I'm being watched. Instead, I continue to peruse the store, walking from one display to the next, picking up my pace with each step and weaving through people.

I'm nearly to the front of the shop when a crowd of about fifteen people filter through the double doors. Perfect. I know it's rude as hell, but I walk straight into the throng of people, pushing my way through, ignoring the glares thrown my way.

When I finally stumble outside, I don't waste any time hightailing it down the street. I duck into the nearest alley I find and slip behind a large dumpster. I pull a few pallets in front of the opening between the wall and the dumpster, effectively barricading myself in.

I've never been thankful for my brief time on the streets until this moment. It taught me how to hide and how to stay put in unpleasant places for long periods of time, which is exactly what I'm planning to do now.

Plus, if whoever is looking for me runs down the alley, I have cover and a clear shot. Damn straight I have my gun on me. I've never had to use it, but I carry around the small pistol like a security blanket, which probably says a lot about me as a person.

It only takes a few moments before I see two large men running by the alley where I'm hiding. The first man runs past, continuing on his pursuit, but the second one stops. I hold my breath and watch as he slowly turns, tilts his head to the side, and breathes in deep. It's creepy as fuck and reminds me of a beast sniffing out his prey.

My clammy hands tighten around my gun, but I don't shoot. The man hasn't made a move yet, he's still just standing at the end of the alley, no doubt taking stock of the potential hiding places.

I can see his sharp, severe features from where I'm crouching, but it's his black eyes that send a shiver down my spine. I guess I was holding on to some hope that maybe it was Luca who found me, but one look at the man now making his way towards me dashes those hopes.

"Come out, come out, wherever you are," he sing-songs in a sinister voice. He's still looking around, but he seems to know I'm here. Fuck. "Ernesto wants you, which means there's no hiding. Seems you have a long-standing debt and he's figured out the perfect way for you to pay him back."

Well, I guess that answers my question about who found me.

I watch the man kick over a stack of crates and curse to himself. He turns around and locks eyes on the lumpy blue tarp a few feet in front of my hiding spot. The man stomps on the tarp hard enough to splash mud on the pallets blocking me in.

I raise my gun and take a deep breath, pulling the trigger on the exhale.

"What the fuck?!" He shouts, falling to the ground. The bullet only grazed the meaty part of his calf, but it was enough to have him writhing on the ground in pain. I kick the pallets in front of me, letting the splintered wood fall right on the asshole's face before leaping over him and making a run for it.

I feel a large hand wrap around my ankle, making me fall and hit the ground hard. I kick wildly as both of us wrestle for the gun I dropped. My foot makes contact with the guy's face, but he only tightens his grip and yanks on my leg, pulling me further away from the gun while he surges forward.

Right before he reaches it, however, police sirens blare from the other end of the alley. Soon the narrow space is lit up with red and blue lights. Shit. I didn't think about how a gunshot at ten in the morning would cause a bit of a scene. Of course, the fucking cops were called.

"Fuck," the man grunts, pushing himself up on his good leg. I use the opportunity to stand up as well, grabbing the gun before he gets the chance. The man shoves me, causing me to stumble backward and smack my head on the unforgiving brick wall. "This isn't over, bitch," he snarls.

My vision goes spotty for a second, but I'm aware of him sprinting away, leaving me to face the cops who are now coming at me with their own guns raised. I suppose a jail cell is better than whatever fate my uncle has for me.

"Put the gun down and get on your knees with your hands behind your head," one cop commands. I do as I'm told.

He cuffs me and reads me my rights as another cop picks the gun up and slips it into an evidence bag.

"I don't suppose this gun is registered, is it?" The cop holding the evidence bag asks. I glare at him, letting him know I'm exercising my right to remain silent. Of course it's not registered. The serial number is scratched off, too.

"Grab the bag, too," the other cop barks at his partner before pulling me up and gripping my upper arm, dragging me towards the police cruiser.

Shit. My laptop and external hard drive are in there. I mean, I know I'm already fucked, but if they break into my computer, I'll be going away for a lot more than firing an unregistered gun.

I'm shoved roughly into the back of the vehicle, hitting my head on the frame of the car, causing me to whimper in pain. The cop sneers at me before slamming the door shut.

I lean my head against the window, forcing myself not to cry as the car weaves its way through the ever-present New York traffic, carrying me to the next chapter of my life.

Chapter 17

Luca

"She's in *jail*?" I yell into the phone for the third time since Matteo called.

I can't fucking believe it. Actually, I can believe it. This is Freya we're talking about, after all. But I still hate the fact she's been alone in a prison cell for a whole day.

"Yes, she's in jail," Matteo confirms.

When I came back to the compound without Freya last week, Darlene broke down into sobs and yelled at Matteo for not letting me go to her sooner. I yelled at him too, but I'm under no illusion my words meant anything. It was all Darlene. Matteo was completely stricken by her tears and apologized profusely before carrying her up to their room.

I don't know what Darlene said to him, but since that night, Matteo has dedicated all of his resources towards finding Freya. He had a meeting with the inner circle and let them know in no uncertain terms that Freya is above suspicion, and should anyone have a problem with that, he'd personally ensure they'd find their way to an early grave. Why he didn't do so when I told him to is unclear, but I'm just grateful Darlene got through to him.

Matteo had all her personal details, history, and electronic paper trails wiped off every database his team of hackers could find. It was clear she tried to cover her tracks before bailing, and although she's good, Matteo's men are better.

We were able to track her to New York two days ago, which is where I've been. I had no fucking clue where to even begin looking for Freya, but I sure as hell couldn't stay in Chicago and just wait for more information. I'm guessing Matteo's men recently got ahold of Freya's arrest record, hence the call from him.

"Luca!" Matteo snaps. "Are you listening?"

"Yeah," I grunt. "I am now."

"I called in a favor with the Gambino's. They have a good number of cops in their pocket and assured me Freya would be out within the hour. She's being held at the station in the forty-fourth precinct. It's in the Bronx."

"Forty-fourth precinct," I repeat, already hailing a cab. I'll have to request a meeting with the Don to thank him for helping us out. The Moscatelli's and the Gambino's only recently formed an alliance, and I'm grateful they were willing to grant us favors so early on.

"Go get your girl, Luca. I, uh, I'm sorry I let the job cloud my judgment."

I pull my phone away from my ear and stare at it, double-checking that I'm still talking to Matteo. I don't think he's ever apologized before. I'm not sure if I forgive him yet, but knowing he feels like an ass helps a little bit.

"Tell her that when I bring her back." I don't give him a chance to respond before hanging up and directing the driver to the police station.

Twenty-five agonizing minutes later, I'm running up the steps and bursting through the doors of the station. "Freya Murphy," I bark at the young guy sitting behind the counter at the front of the station. His eyes go wide, and I'm sure he's thankful for the bullet-proof window separating us right about now. Clearly, he's a rookie who got stuck with the shitty desk job.

"Uh, what? I-I mean, are you looking for —"

"Freya Murphy," I say slowly, trying to get myself under control. The last thing I need is to be thrown into a cell because I couldn't keep my anger under control. "She was arrested yesterday. I'm here to pick her up."

The young guy clicks around on the computer and then not so subtly ticks his eyes between me and the screen.

"There a problem?" I prompt.

"Uh, just let me go get my sergeant," he rushes to say before scampering off. The kid's not going to cut it as a cop, I can already tell.

I pace around the little office area, running my fingers through my hair and rubbing the back of my neck. I know I can't very well storm through the station and break her out myself, but I swear to God, I'll come back with an army of Gambino men and…

"Luca?"

I spin around on my heel at the sound of her soft, timid voice. As soon as she sees me, Freya runs and jumps into my arms, wrapping her legs around me and burying her face into the side of my neck.

Just as quickly, however, she tries wiggling out of my embrace. I hold her tighter. No way am I letting her go any time soon.

"I've got you, baby girl. I'm right here."

"You're not angry?" She whispers.

"Angry? No. Worried out of my goddamn mind is more like it. Fuck, Freya, you can't ever leave me again." I feel her nod her head from where it's tucked into the crook of my shoulder.

Our moment is interrupted by the skittish rookie cop, who hands me Freya's backpack. The kid's hands are shaking. I grab the bag and sling it over my shoulder, not bothering with paperwork or whatever since I know the police are going to forget about ever having Freya arrested in the first place.

She clings to me until I finally have to set her down to hail another cab, but I keep an arm around her and tuck her trembling body into my side.

Once we're in the cab, I pull her onto my lap and hold her while she cries. I direct the driver to The Plaza, where the Gambino's set me up in the penthouse suite, and then rock Freya back and forth in my arms in that comforting gesture I know she loves.

Finally, after what feels like forever, but I know was only about half an hour, we pull into the luxury hotel. Freya gets out of the cab and starts walking towards the entrance, but I won't have any of that. I scoop her up in my arms, right where she's meant to be.

My precious girl doesn't even protest. It kills me to think of what this week has been like for her. She has no fight left, only heartbreak. I swear I can feel the agony radiating off her soft, sweet skin.

I carry Freya to the private elevator that only goes to the penthouse, and then walk through the rooms until I get to the master suite, finally depositing her on the bed before crawling in beside her. I wrap my body around Freya, my front to her back, and cover her broken pieces with my own, knowing we'll fit together and be whole once more.

We lie there in silence for a while, until Freya finally speaks.

"Why are you here? Don't you hate me?"

Jesus, her words gut me. "I could never hate you, Freya. I love you. I love you so fucking much. I don't know everything about you and your past, but I want to. I'll protect you, all of you, and I'll guard your secrets with my life. I just need to know what they are. I can't protect you if I don't even know what the threat is."

Freya turns in my arms so we're face to face. She pierces me with her stare, and I watch as she wrestles with doubt, despair, regret, and finally a sorrowful, wistful hope. My beautiful Freya is tormented not only by her past but by her future as well. I can see it all in those clear green eyes of hers. She really thought she'd spend the rest of her life alone, away from the people who love her most in the world, and she can't quite believe I'm here and I still want her.

She reaches out to cup my cheek, and I turn my head to kiss her palm. I notice angry red marks on her skin from her nails, a habit Freya has when she's scared or anxious. I have to tamp down my rage at the visual reminder of how much pain and heartbreak she's been through this last week. Hell, her entire life.

"Why would you protect me if you think I'm the mole?"

"I don't think you're a spy," I tell her adamantly. I reach out and trail my fingers over her temple, her cheek, her jaw, and down her neck, just like the first time we kissed. She's still a mystery to me in many ways, but I'm more determined than ever to spend the rest of my life figuring her out.

"You...you don't?"

"I didn't believe that for a single second, *la mia anima*. We haven't known each other very long, but I *know* you, Freya. I feel you in every cell of my body. I crave you with every breath in my lungs. I love you with every beat of my heart. I always will. I promise we'll get through this, but I have to know what you're running from."

I wipe her tears away and then press my lips to her forehead, lingering there while I breathe her in. Even after spending twenty-four hours in a jail cell, she still smells like lavender and saltwater and *mine*.

"You already know a little bit about my dad," she starts, her voice soft and tentative. I nod, pulling back from her a little so I can see her face. "He was always a bit...off, I guess. I knew he struggled with all kinds of addictions, but he was able to keep it together while my stepmom, Isabella, was around. After she died, it was like he no longer had a reason to fight those demons."

Freya shrugs like it's no big deal, but I hear the words she didn't say out loud. She wasn't a good enough reason for him to stay sober, and she carries that weight around with her to this day.

"I'm sorry you never had the love you needed, baby girl. I promise I'll love you enough to make up for the pain others caused you in the past."

Freya sniffles as a fresh wave of tears stream down her face. I wipe them away and cup the back of her neck, keeping her close and massaging her sore, tight muscles while she gathers her thoughts.

"I'm sure you know by now Ernesto Mazzi is my step-uncle." I nod, and she winces, but I don't let her pull away from me. "I only met him once while Isabella was alive, but he started coming around a lot more after she died. He always frightened me, so I hid in my room whenever he came over. I figured out later that Ernesto was hooking my dad up with loans for gambling, or drinking, or drugs, or whatever destructive behavior he was into. Of course, my dad had no way to pay him back, but I assume that was all part of Ernesto's plan.

"When my dad inevitably couldn't come up with the money by the deadline, Ernesto told him he could work his debt off and get more money by "running errands". It started out with little things – sneaking into places to steal paperwork, sitting in a designated seat in a restaurant with a recording device to pick up on intel from whoever he was told to spy on, stuff like that. Ernesto kept giving him money, so Dad kept running errands. The tasks became bigger, though. More dangerous. He needed more than one person, so he started taking me along."

"Oh, Freya," I murmur, kissing her forehead again. "How old were you?"

"Thirteen," she shrugs, trying to brush it off. Even when she's baring her soul to me, she doesn't want to acknowledge her own pain. I know that will come soon enough. No one can carry around heavy shit like this and not break at some point. I want to be there when it happens so I can keep her from drowning in an ocean of sorrow.

"He sent me on some of the more dangerous assignments, saying no one would expect a kid to spy or steal things. Turns out, I'm not good at being quiet and sneaky," she snorts out a sad, bitter laugh. "I ended up in juvie for a few months when I got caught stealing something for my dad."

"After I got out, he told me I still had to earn my keep, so I taught myself how to hack into databases, bank accounts, and other places so my dad could take on bigger missions and earn more money to throw away on drugs and hookers. I knew what we were doing was wrong, and I think I knew even then we were working for someone far more important than my sketchy step-uncle, but I still trusted my dad for some stupid reason."

"It's not stupid, Freya. He was your family. I loved my mom even though she continually brought monsters home to live with us. That's just how it is sometimes."

Freya nods, her eyes meeting mine once again. "My dad was arrested a few times for minor offenses, which was how I ended up in foster care on and off for a few years. When I was sixteen, though, he got himself in too deep. I still don't know if it was money or a botched 'errand', but Ernesto sent some men to our trailer to threaten and rough up my dad. The men said he had until the end of the week to 'make it right', whatever that meant. By then I had figured out we were all tied up with the Ricci family, so I knew the threats on my dad's life weren't idle."

"I still remember my dad's response word for word. *Take my daughter as a peace offering. Tell Ernesto to give her to the Don or sell her off. She's untouched, she'll make a pretty penny.*"

"Fuck!" I bark out, making Freya jump. "Sorry," I say, trying to make my voice softer so as not to startle her again. But holy fucking shit is it hard to not throw the desk in the corner out of the goddamn window in an attempt to work out my anger. I'm not okay. None of this is okay. But I need to hear the rest.

"That's when I left. I didn't think about it. Hell, I didn't even take anything with me, I just snuck out my window and ran. I slept out on the streets for two weeks before a cop found me and told me my dad was dead. Apparently, he didn't have anything else the Ricci's wanted, so they made good on their threat."

"And that's when you met Darlene?"

Freya nods and smiles, but then the tears start again. "Darlene. Does she hate me?"

"Not at all," I reassure her. "I don't think you realize just how loved you are, Freya. We're all worried about you and we need you." I brush a soft kiss on her lips and encourage her to keep telling me her story. I want to know every single thing about this incredible woman in my arms.

"I was paranoid for a while, but I convinced myself the men who were there that night didn't even know what I looked like. I hoped since I hadn't seen Ernesto in over a decade, he wouldn't recognize me, either. I didn't even know if my step-uncle heard about my dad's offer to sell me, so I guess I got lulled into a false sense of security."

"But then you noticed you were being followed," I say more to myself than to Freya, remembering the scare she had in the parking lot. Fuck, I wonder if she had another scare the night of the rehearsal dinner when she came back all shaky and nervous.

"Yeah. I mean, I tried to reason with myself that it's been years since all of the stuff with my dad went down, and if Ernesto didn't bother to find me yet, maybe I was in the clear."

"Do you know how Ernesto got you on his radar after all this time?"

Freya rolls onto her back and sighs. "I've been trying to figure that out. The only thing I can think of is that he found out the connection between Darlene and I when she was kidnapped. I'm guessing the fact that I was associated with the Moscatelli family made me even more appealing to the Ricci's.

"Two guys found me yesterday while I was out. One of them cornered me and confirmed my suspicions; I still had to pay my father's debt."

"You were cornered? Yesterday? Did they hurt you?" I sit up and examine Freya for scrapes and bruises, but she just shakes her head no. Jesus, I was so focused on getting her out of the police station and into my arms, I didn't even ask how she was arrested in the first place.

"I'm fine. I shot the guy, though," she smirks. Fuck, it's good to see her feisty personality shine through.

"That's my girl," I smile at her and nuzzle her neck, breathing her in once again.

"I only got him in the leg. The cops showed up in record time after the gun went off, and the asshole got away. I was left standing there with the smoking gun – literally. And then, well, you know the rest."

"Yeah," I nod, still processing everything Freya just told me. Ernesto isn't going to give her up easily, but neither will I. He wants to take what's mine? He'll pay with his life. Matteo is right – war's coming. And I have a bullet with Ernesto's name on it.

I start to sit up, but Freya grabs my arm in a death grip.

"Please don't leave," she whimpers, her voice cracking with emotion. "I'm sorry. I overheard the conversation about finding the mole and someone accusing Darlene and then me, and I didn't want you or Darlene to be associated with me. I knew what you would find and how guilty I would look. Please, please believe me. Don't leave," she begs.

"I'm not leaving, baby girl," I promise as I gently tug my arm out of her grasp and stand up. She looks up at me with watery eyes as I start stripping off my clothes.

I kneel beside her on the bed in just my boxer briefs and help her sit up so I can peel her dress off. Freya lets me but continues to stare at me in confusion. I lay her back down and hold her, curling my body around hers with nothing in the way this time.

"I needed to feel you," I whisper into the back of her neck before kissing her there. I stroke my hand up and down her soft curves and ghost my lips back and forth over her bare shoulder. Freya turns to face me and cups my cheek.

She leans in close, her lips only an inch from mine. "I need you, too," she whispers. "I need all of you. Please?"

Chapter 18

Freya

Luca's piercing blue eyes reflect the same longing and desperate need I'm feeling. I still can't believe he came for me. I have no idea how or why, but I don't give a fuck. He's here. And he still loves me, even after everything I put him through.

"Please?" I whisper again, my lips brushing his when I speak.

Luca closes the distance between us, kissing me softly, taking his time to taste me, and explore my mouth. It's so sweet and tender I feel like I might break down into tears for the tenth time today.

"Please…" I whimper, pressing my body against his and trailing my hands up his bare chest. God, I never thought I'd see him again, let alone touch him. I need more.

"I've got you, *la mia anima*. I know what you need," he murmurs. Luca gives me one last kiss and then gets out of bed. Before I even get a chance to protest, he lifts me up in his arms and carries me towards the bathroom, kissing me the whole way there.

As soon as he sets me down, Luca turns the water on in the massive, luxurious shower. Water pours out from a rainfall showerhead, as well as *two* other shower heads on either side of the shower. Why would anyone need this setup? Rich people. Fucking weird, every last one of them.

"What are you thinking about?" Luca asks from behind me as he unclasps my bra. He trails his fingers up my back, pushing the straps down my shoulders and kissing me there.

"Just wondering why rich people need multiple shower heads."

Luca chuckles darkly, making me shiver. "I guess we'll have to find out."

He helps me into the shower once we're both naked, and positions me right in the middle of the multiple streams. I close my eyes and let the hot water trickle over my skin. I can't help the sigh that escapes my lips. "Okay. This is pretty nice," I admit.

"I think we can do better than nice," Luca murmurs. I open my eyes and see him standing right in front of me, his normally blue eyes a stormy gray.

His fingertips follow the streams of water as they pour over my shoulders, my breasts, my torso, my hips, and finally my throbbing pussy. I moan as his knuckles barely graze my mound before continuing down my inner thighs.

Luca's other hand wraps around the back of my neck, pulling me in for a punishing kiss. I open up for him, needing to taste and touch and feel him everywhere. He tugs my hair, pulling my head back so he can deepen the kiss. I feel two fingers dip into my slit and start circling my little bundle of nerves in slow, steady strokes.

I grip his biceps, digging my nails in as one finger pushes into my entrance, then two. Luca thrusts his large digits in and out of me, slowly at first, and then faster, faster, faster, grinding his heel down on my clit all while devouring my lips.

Breaking the kiss, I bury my face in between his neck and shoulders as I cry out. I'm *right* there, so close to my much needed release. He keeps pumping his fingers, twisting and curling them up to rub against my G-spot. Again, again, one more time…

Suddenly, his hand is gone. I nearly fall over at the loss of him, but I regain my composure and glare right at his stupidly handsome face. Luca just grins, which makes my pussy clench. God, this man. Frustrating, sweet, and sexy as hell.

"Not yet, baby girl. Patience."

With that, he spins me around, my back to his front, and starts massaging me everywhere. I feel his large, calloused hands squeezing my breasts, my hips, my soft, round belly that I've always been a little self-conscious of. Luca has made it clear that he loves every inch of me.

His hands trail lower, once again teasing my pussy lips. My clit throbs in time with my heartbeat, begging him to do something about the unbearable ache he's created.

"Luca…" I moan, wiggling my hips in an attempt to get him to touch me where I need him most.

"Not yet," he murmurs again, licking the shell of my ear before trailing kisses down my neck and shoulder.

I feel his hard cock dig into my ass, so I wiggle a bit more until I feel his length nestle in between my cheeks. Luca groans and rotates his hips, grinding his thick shaft against my ass.

"God, please, Luca," I beg. My legs start shaking, and I have to lean forward and brace myself against the wall.

A low growl rises up from deep in Luca's chest, the sound vibrating through me, nearly making me come on the spot. He grips my left leg just under my knee and lifts it so my foot is resting on a bench in the corner of the shower I didn't notice earlier.

"That's it, fuck, love when you're spread out for me, baby girl." He continues touching every inch of me, caressing my thighs and widening my stance a bit. "Now let's see what I can do to convince you we need this set up at home."

"Home," I whisper, unable to stop the tide of emotion that rolls over me at the word.

"Home," Luca repeats. "With me. Always."

"Always," I nod in agreement.

Luca gives me a satisfied grunt, which makes me giggle. My laughter is cut off when I feel his cock slide up and down my slit. He taps my clit, nearly sending me over the edge. I'm so damn sensitive and ready to come I think I might die if he doesn't get inside of me this second.

"I've got you, Freya," he murmurs, lining himself up with my entrance.

I'm expecting him to thrust inside of me and fuck me hard. I know he's as desperate for me as I am for him. But Luca slowly inches inside of me, prolonging the sweet pain deep in my core. He grips my hips, holding me in place as he stretches me open. I hold my breath as he slides home, hitting the very end of me.

"Fucking Christ," he whispers. "I've missed you so damn much."

Luca pulls out, just as slowly, making me whine. I open my mouth to tell him to fuck me already, but then Luca slams his thick dick all the way inside, making me come instantly.

He wraps his arms around me, holding me up as I spasm around his cock. He fucks me through it, hammering into me over and over, as I continue to convulse and cry out his name. I feel Luca grip my inner thigh of my leg that's propped up, spreading me wider and angling my hips so he's hitting my G-spot with every thrust.

"Y-y-yesss…" I manage to hiss out as I pound my fist against the wall and throw my head back against his shoulder. Luca wraps his hand around my throat, keeping my head tilted back as he splits me open with his dick.

"So fucking tight for me, love," he grits out.

I whimper in response, already feeling another orgasm rushing to the surface. He must sense it, too. Luca keeps a firm grip on my neck, which is hot as fuck, and then trails his other hand down my body, circling my clit and then pinching it.

My orgasm slams into me, hard and fast, ripping a scream from my lips. Luca growls and ruts into me, rubbing furious circles over my swollen, pulsing clit. A painful, delicious pleasure takes over every part of my body as I come again for him, sobbing his name.

Luca pulls out and spins me around, crashing his lips down on mine as he lifts me up and spears me with his cock. I wrap my legs around his hips and hang on for dear life as he pins me to the wall and fucks me like a man possessed.

"Mine, mine, fucking *mine*. Say it, Freya. Tell me, baby girl."

"Y-yours," I whisper, my voice scratchy from screaming his name.

"Louder," he growls.

"I'm yours!" I cry out, writhing in his arms.

Luca roars and bites my shoulder as he comes, marking me, claiming me, fucking me raw. I gasp and open my mouth in a silent scream, my entire body pulsing, tensing, stretching...and then collapsing in on itself as my orgasm ravishes me from the inside out.

I swear I feel Luca come again, shooting his cum deep inside of me in forceful bursts.

I drag air into my lungs in short breaths, trembling in Luca's arms as he keeps me pinned to the wall. I comb my fingers through his hair while he nuzzles into my shoulder, kissing over the spot where he bit me.

"Fuck, are you okay? I bit you," he says in shock.

"Yeah, you did," I grin. "And it was hot as fuck."

Luca looks up at me, his eyes going dark as a deep growl rumbles through him. I think he might fuck me again, but then his eyes turn soft, and he kisses my forehead.

"Let's get you washed up so you can rest. Then I'll do it all over again."

My pussy clenches around his half hard cock, making Luca groan. "Or we could do it again right now..."

Luca sucks in a breath and lets it out slowly, resting his forehead on mine. "Do you trust me?"

I nod automatically. Of course, I trust him. The man keeps showing up and getting me out of my messes and proving to me I can have a happily ever after, too.

"Then let me take care of you."

I nod again as he gently sets me down and begins washing me. Luca's touch is achingly tender like I'm precious to him and he wants to savor every moment of being with me like this. I can't stop the tears stinging my eyes. Luca doesn't say anything, he just kisses them away and continues washing my body before moving on to my hair.

Luca dries me off with a fluffy towel and then scoops me up in his arms again, making me giggle. "I can walk, you know." Even as I say it though, I snuggle deeper into his arms.

"I know, baby. You can do anything you want. And I think you want me to hold you as much as possible."

I don't bother arguing with him. He's right. I want as much of him as possible. We've only been apart for a week, but it felt like a lifetime. I think we'll be making up for lost time for weeks to come.

Even though it's the middle of the day, we curl up in bed, under the warm, soft covers. Sleep pulls at the corners of my mind, but it's not until Luca kisses my forehead and tucks me into his side that I finally drift off.

Chapter 19

Luca

A sharp, loud knock yanks me from my sleep, making me growl. I bury my face deeper into Freya's messy hair and pull her closer to me, but the knocking starts again, more frantic this time.

"What's going on?" Freya asks, her voice thick with sleep. "Is everything okay?"

I reach for my phone and see that it's barely seven in the morning. Freya and I flew into Chicago last night and crashed as soon as we got home. Matteo made me promise to bring Freya over for breakfast first thing in the morning so Darlene could see her and make sure she's okay. I guess "first thing in the morning" wasn't an exaggeration.

"Time to get up, baby. Darlene's here to make sure you're alive."

"Leena!" Freya hops out of bed, but I grab her around her waist and pull her back down. She squeals as I roll on top of her and pin her beneath me. God, I love this woman. Her green eyes sparkle with light and playfulness, and fuck, do I want to play with her.

"You didn't give me a good morning kiss," I grunt, bending down to capture her lips. Freya jerks her head to the side at the last minute, making me growl.

"I have morning breath," she hisses.

I cup her chin and turn her face towards me once again. "Do you think I give a fuck about morning breath?" She shakes her head no. "Good."

With that, I claim her mouth, drinking down her sweet flavor. Morning breath? This woman is crazy. But I already knew that. In fact, it's one of the things I love most about her.

"Freya Murphy! Get your butt out here!" Darlene yells while banging on the front door again.

"Calm your tits, Leena, I need to put some clothes on!" Freya shouts back.

"I really wish you wouldn't," I murmur, kissing down her neck.

"Freya!" Darlene calls out, making me groan. "You almost burst in on Matteo and me when I first came back, and now I'm returning the favor."

"You almost walked in on Matteo and Darlene?" I ask.

"Chill out, Luca. You're the only Moscatelli family member I want to see naked," she sasses, rolling her eyes at me.

"I better be the only person you want to see naked, period," I grunt before kissing her breathless.

"Seriously! Five minutes, missy, or else I'm gonna pull my gun out!"

Freya giggles at Darlene's threat. "Leena, I think all that power is going to your head."

"Then you better come out here and give me a talking to." The girls laugh at their own banter, which makes me smile. I'm glad they'll always have each other.

Reluctantly, I get out of bed and help Freya find some clothes. "Have fun with Darlene, baby girl," I tell her, kissing her on the temple. "Don't get into too much trouble."

Freya turns her head and kisses my cheek. "But if I do, I'll just call you," she winks.

"Damn right you will," I whisper, kissing the side of her neck before spinning her around and giving her juicy ass a playful smack. "I'll probably be with Matteo and some other guys for most of the day, but I promise to be home for dinner."

"Is someone else going to be making that dinner?" She smirks. "I already cooked for you once this month. I'm no kept woman, you know."

"But you'll let me keep you?"

Freya narrows her eyes, trying so hard to look indignant, but failing in the cutest way possible. I close the distance between us and wrap her up in my arms, kissing her all over her beautiful face. She giggles and squirms, but I hold her close and nibble on her bottom lip before diving in and devouring her.

When we break apart for air, Freya rests her forehead on mine. "Yeah. I'll let you keep me, Luca. But I get to keep you, too."

"Always, love. I'm yours."

Darlene pounds on the front door again, making me groan, and Freya laugh. "I better go out there or she's going to send in the heavy hitters."

"Nah. *Darlene* is the heavy hitter."

Freya snorts out a laugh before skipping to the front door. It's going to be a long, painful couple of hours before I can see her again.

✳✳✳

"Are you fucking kidding me? You're sending me out to collect a mafia princess?" Rocco practically whines when I tell him about his next assignment.

"Do you have a problem with that?" Matteo asks, stepping into my office.

"No, boss. Of course not."

"Good."

"It's just…"

Matteo glares at him with one eyebrow raised, daring Rocco to continue.

"It seems like maybe someone else would be better suited for the job? I mean Alessia is what, eighteen? And about as big as my pinky finger. Plus, she hasn't left the Ricci family mansion pretty much her whole life. I'm just saying, she doesn't seem like a threat. At least, not one that requires my skill set, you know, boss?"

"Are you too good for this assignment? Am I going to regret promoting you at such a young age?"

"No, boss. Of course not. I was just asking."

"Well stop asking," Matteo grunts.

Rocco bows his head, which almost makes me crack a grin. The six-foot-seven mountain of a man is eager and a bit hot-headed, but he respects Matteo with every cell in his body. I'm not sure what the story is between them, but it's clear his loyalty is always with Matteo.

"Anything else, boss?" Rocco asks.

"That's it. Check in with Luca once you have Alessia in tow."

Rocco nods, and for a brief second, I think the guy is going to curtsey or some shit, but he turns around instead, closing the door behind him.

Matteo sighs heavily. "Am I screwing up by sending him out there to collect Alessia Ricci?"

"Rocco's a good kid, he just needs to think before he speaks sometimes."

Matteo nods his head. "It's a big assignment and he's so much younger than everyone else in the inner circle."

"You were thirty when you took over the family," I remind him. "Rocco is what, twenty-nine?"

"Something like that," Matteo grunts. "You're right, though. He's got a good head on his shoulders and his heart is the right place. I just need to remind him your word is as good as mine when it comes to handing down assignments."

Matteo pauses for a moment, looking away from me. If I didn't know any better, I'd think he was nervous, but that can't be right.

"Look," he finally speaks again, rubbing a hand over the back of his neck. "I'm not good at this apology shit, but I just got done apologizing to Freya, and Darlene said I need to apologize to you, too. Even after I told her I already did." Matteo is practically pouting as he says the last few words. Who would have thought the intimidating mafia boss would be going around apologizing to anyone and everyone Darlene points her finger at?

"Alright then. I'm ready to hear your apology." I know I shouldn't be enjoying this as much as I am, but hell, he's more than earned whatever shit I give him. Matteo knows it too, even though he's glaring at me.

"I have reasons why I pushed so hard to investigate Freya, especially while in the company of others. I can't explain everything yet, but I will when Alessia gets here and can confirm a few of my suspicions. However, it was never my goal to send Freya running or to put her in harm's way. I meant what I told you before, I thought I was protecting her. But that doesn't mean I don't feel like shit for practically handing her over to the Ricci's."

My jaw tenses at the thought of Freya running into Ricci's men, of them scaring her and hurting her. Thank fuck she's okay. I hate not having her in my sight right now, but she needs time with Darlene, and Matteo and I need to discuss what to do next.

Matteo sits down across from me, resting his elbows on his knees. "I'm sorry, Luca. I remember how fucked up I was when Darlene was missing, and I can't imagine what it was like for you to experience that torture for a whole week."

I look away from him, trying to breathe through the sudden tightness in my chest. It was the worst thing I've ever experienced, which is saying something. I don't think I could survive something like that again. I can't speak yet, so I just nod.

"I always have your back, Luca. Both you and Freya. Darlene has Freya's back too, which honestly carries more weight than my promise of protection these days," he shakes his head.

I can't help but grin a little at that. "Yeah, your woman came to our house today and threatened to use her gun on me if Freya didn't come to the door."

Matteo chuckles and I join him. "We've got our hands full, don't we?"

"We sure do. But I wouldn't have it any other way."

"Same here. Are we done sharing our feelings and shit?"

I chuckle again and shake my head. "Yeah. You can tell Darlene to let you out of the dog house."

"Oh, thank fuck. She's merciless when she wants to be." Matteo says it like he's annoyed, but the smile on his face tells me he loves being bossed around by his woman. I get it. I like being bossed around by mine, too.

"We good here? I've got my own bossy woman waiting for me at home."

"We're good," he confirms. "Go spend some time with Freya. Let me know when you hear from Rocco and we'll figure out a plan from there."

"Whatever you need, boss. I'm ready for war. No one threatens my woman and lives to tell about it. Ernesto is mine." I hold Matteo's gaze until he nods his head. He knows what I mean. The kill is mine. My bullet will be the one to end his life.

We shake hands before Matteo leaves my office. I check my phone and see it's nearly six in the evening. Is that dinner time? I promised her I'd be home for dinner. Damn, I hope I didn't piss Freya off.

I laugh at myself as I collect my things and head out for the day. A month ago, the idea of pissing Freya off would have brought me a sense of smug satisfaction. Now, I only want her smiles. Okay, I want her fight and fury, too. I love that side of her. But more than anything, I just want Freya to be happy.

Less than ten minutes later, I'm pulling up to the house. Our house. Fuck, I like the sound of that. I can't stop myself from running up the porch steps and flinging the front door open.

I almost freak out when I don't see her on the couch or in the kitchen, but then I hear Larry bark. Yes, I know the different barks from the dogs – even the cat who thinks he's a dog. And yes, he barks, too.

The sound is coming from our bedroom, so that's the direction I head. When I open the door, I see my beautiful Freya snuggled up under a pile of blankets, snoring softly while the dogs watch over her. Larry is the only one awake enough to greet me, but even so, he doesn't leave Freya's side. Good boy.

I walk over and pick him up, along with Curly, who is fast asleep. Mo, never one to be left out, follows his brothers and me out to the kitchen so I can feed them. Hopefully, their dinner will be enough to keep them distracted for a while. I have some plans for my precious girl.

Once the mutts have full food and water bowls, I head back to the bedroom, strip down, and crawl in behind Freya, wrapping my arms around her and pulling her back to my front. God, this is all I wanted; all I thought about the entire damn day.

"Luca?" She whispers all sleepy and sexy as fuck.

"Yes, *la mia anima*?"

"Missed you." Freya yawns and snuggles closer, brushing her ass against my already hardening cock.

"Missed you too, baby girl," I whisper, kissing the back of her neck. She wiggles again, making me groan. "Careful," I warn. The little minx does it again, this time purposefully grinding down on my now painfully hard dick.

"I'm not known for my cautious nature," she purrs.

"Jesus, woman, I wasn't planning on fucking you as soon as I got home." Even as I say it though, my hand slides down the front of the oversized t-shirt she's wearing, and I cup her hot little pussy through the fabric.

"You say that, but you're the one who crawled in here all naked and whatnot." Freya looks at me over her shoulder and bites her bottom lip before giving me a wicked smile. "I, on the other hand, practiced much more restraint. After getting out of the shower, I threw one of your shirts on."

A low growl leaves my throat. "Do you have anything else on underneath this shirt?"

"Why don't you find out?"

I crash my lips down on hers and slip my hand under the shirt she's wearing, groaning when my fingers brush across her bare pussy. Her bare, dripping wet, hot little pussy.

"Jesus," I groan. "Did you have some dirty dreams while you were sleeping, baby girl?"

Freya gasps as I dip a finger into her soaking entrance, stroking in and out of her slowly, gathering up her juices and circling her clit.

"Yesss…" she hisses out as I continue to rub lazy circles over her bundle of nerves. Freya rocks her hips and grinds down on my hand, the motion inching her shirt higher and higher until her ass is exposed to me.

I grip her top leg and drape it over mine, opening her up for me. She tries pushing back, but I grip her hip to keep her in place while slowly sliding my hard length through her folds. Freya's pussy lips flutter around me, trying to suck me in, but I continue my shallow thrusts, tapping her clit with the head of my cock.

"Luca!" She whimpers, grabbing my hand that's resting on her hip. Her nails dig into my flesh, making me growl. "Please, please, I need it."

"Fuck," I grunt. "You know I'll always give you what you need."

With that, I pull back and thrust inside of her, rolling my hips to find that one spot I know gives her the most pleasure.

"Holy fucking shit!" She screams, thrashing around in my arms.

"There it is," I grunt, hitting it again and again while sliding my hand up her torso to grab her breast. I pull and pinch her hard nipple, causing Freya to bow her back and press her ass further into me.

We both cry out as she meets me thrust for thrust, wedging my thick dick further inside of her. Jesus, her pussy is so tight, so fucking wet for me. I never thought I'd get to experience pleasure like this, and fuck knows I don't deserve to have Freya in my life at all, let alone be inside of her every fucking chance I get, but I'm a selfish bastard and she's mine. Freya is all mine.

Her cunt clenches around me as wet smacking noises fill the air, joining our labored breaths and broken cries. Freya reaches out behind her to grab my hair, clinging to me as I pound into her over and over.

"L-L-Lucaaaa, oh God, ohmygod, I...I'm..."

"Come for me. Come on my big fat cock, baby girl. I want to feel it," I growl, holding her in place while I hammer into her and give my woman what she needs. Her ass jiggles with each forceful thrust, the sight nearly sending me over the edge. But I bite back my orgasm, needing her to get there first.

Freya tenses and holds her breath, her entire body wound so tight she's shaking. Her pussy clamps down on me so fucking hard as my woman lets go of every-fucking-thing and comes for me. She absolutely drenches my dick with her release.

Satisfied with having one orgasm out of the way, I pull out and roll over on my back, then pull Freya on top of me, positioning her so she's straddling my lap.

Goddamn. My woman's hair is an absolute mess, her face is flushed, her chest is heaving, and her entire body trembles as she sits on top of me, trying to catch her breath.

Then she opens her green eyes and grins at me. Fucking grins. Jesus Christ, I'll never get enough of her.

"Ride my fucking cock, Freya."

"Don't tell me what to do," she sasses, rubbing her pussy up and down my length.

"Shit, baby," I groan, running my hands up and down her thighs.

Freya takes off her shirt, revealing her gorgeous body to me. I slide my hands up her torso, taking in every smooth inch of her creamy skin. I love the way it feels under my rough hands. It's overwhelming. This goddess has completely destroyed me and then built me up again, making her the center of my universe. The crazy thing is, she didn't even try.

"I'm dying here, love," I grit out. She grins again and reaches down to palm my cock. I hiss out a breath and bite the side of my cheek to hold back my orgasm. I only want to come inside of her.

She leans forward, spreading her hands out over my chest and raising her hips. Slowly, so fucking slowly, Freya sinks down on my dick. Her eyes close, her lips part and her brow furrows as a look of absolute pleasure takes over her face.

"You're so deep like this," she breathes out.

My dick twitches and leaks precum like a goddamn faucet. I release the breath that was caught in my lungs and grip her hips, helping her find a rhythm she likes. I love getting to explore all of this with her. I might as well have been a virgin when we met, and right now, I couldn't be more grateful for that. Learning each other's bodies, discovering how we fit, how we push, how we pull, how we shatter…it's fucking everything.

Freya leans back, resting her hands on my upper thighs as she grinds down on my dick. I can't stop touching her, feeling her, running my fingers over her curves and soft, silky skin. I twist my hips and scrape my cock against her front wall, making Freya squeeze her thighs and gush all over me.

"You like that?" I ask, doing it again.

"Oh…oh fuck, yes," she moans, the sexy, throaty sound encouraging me to continue. She falls forward, catching herself on her hands, one on either side of my head. I cup the back of her neck and pull her down for a kiss, diving right into her sweet, sexy mouth as our flesh slaps together again and again.

"I feel you, Freya. I know you want to come for me."

She nods and squeezes her pussy around me, sucking me in and rolling her hips. My balls draw up tight, but I hang on, needing her to come again. She swivels her hips, her movements becoming jerky as she nears her end.

I grip her hips in a punishing hold, holding her still while I fuck up into that tight little cunt. Freya rests her sweaty forehead on mine, her red hair making a curtain around us as we grunt and fuck frantically.

"I-I-I can't…can't hold on," she stutters out, her breath caught in her throat as her eyes roll back into her head.

"Then don't. Fucking let go Freya. I've got you. Let go, love, let go," I murmur. Freya stares at me with those devastating green eyes of hers and explodes around me, never breaking eye contact. "That's it, goddamn, come harder for me, baby. Come so fucking hard."

I feel it, feel her pushing herself to give me more of her pleasure, to give me everything she has. Freya screams and throws her head back, squeezing my cock so damn tight as her orgasm devastates her. Feeling her cream all over my dick has me filling her up with my cum, rope after rope until our combined release drips down my balls and pools on the sheet below.

I ease Freya off of me, but instead of letting her roll to the side, I pull her still convulsing pussy up my body, towards my face.

"Wh-what?" She asks, still out of breath and sexy as hell.

"I want to try something."

"Um, okay…"

"Do you trust me?" Freya immediately nods. "Then ride my face."

"Y-you're awfully demanding today," she tries to tease me, but her words slur together in the aftermath of her previous orgasms.

"I think you like it."

Freya narrows her eyes at me but then nods her head. "I think I do, too."

"Good," I smirk. "Now be a good girl and ride my fucking face."

"I...um, but like, your uh, your..." her face turns bright red with whatever thought is on the tip of her tongue. I raise my eyebrows, encouraging her to continue. "Your cum is leaking out of me," she whispers.

I grin and nudge her up towards my head. My mouth is fucking watering for a taste of her. "Good. I want to know how we taste together. Don't you?"

Without waiting for her answer, I swipe two fingers up her slit, gathering up our combined juices and lifting them up to her mouth. Freya opens up for me and sucks on my digits, swirling her tongue around the pads of my fingers.

A growl thunders out of my chest as her eyes go dark with need. I pull my hand away from her mouth and smack her ass until she finally crawls up my body and positions her dripping pussy above my face.

"Like this?" She asks tentatively.

"Fuck. Just like that. Hang on to the headboard, baby girl. I can't control myself any longer."

I grip her hips and pull her down, suffocating on her cunt and lapping up every trace of us. It might be twisted, but I fucking love it. Love tasting us. Love knowing we made this mess. Love cleaning it up with my tongue.

"Oh shit!" Freya squeals. I chuckle into her pussy, making her release more of her sweet cream. "God, Luca, I can't believe we haven't done this before now," she moans.

I grunt and suck on her clit, making her thighs tighten around my head. I'm filled with pride knowing I can bring my woman pleasure like this. I'm the lucky son of a bitch who gets to do this every single day for the rest of our lives.

Freya grinds down on me, letting go of the last of her reserves and giving in to my touch. Her surrender is the greatest, sweetest, most precious gift I could ever ask for. I'll make damn sure she never regrets giving it to me.

One hand remains on her hip, steadying her while my tongue explores her folds, memorizing her pussy and making note of what makes her tremble, what makes her gush, and what makes her cry out my name.

My other hand slides around her ass, gripping the soft flesh and inching closer to her back entrance. I dip a finger in between her cheeks and circle it around her tight ring of muscles. Freya gasps and shudders, but I can tell she likes it from the way her pussy twitches.

"Luca…" She whimpers, pressing her ass back into my hand. Fuck, my girl is as dirty as I am, and it's all new territory for us. I can't wait to discover what other filthy shit we both like.

I gather up her cream and gently massage her puckered little hole, groaning into her pussy when I feel it pulse around me. I roll her clit in between my lips, keeping her *right* there, so close to her release, but not sending her over just yet.

Slowly, I slide one finger into her tight as fuck ass, pumping it in and out. Freya gasps, both of her holes clenching around me as I spear her with my tongue and finger.

"Oh fuck, oh fuck, oh fuck yes," she cries out. Jesus, she's fucking shaking above me, gasping for air and fucking my face like a goddamn porn star.

My Freya inhales sharply and then splinters apart for me, her ass clenching around my finger while her pussy floods my mouth with her release. She squirts her cream into my mouth, making my cock explode. Holy fuck, she didn't even touch my dick, and yet she controls him completely.

Freya shudders out the last of her orgasm as I gently move her off me. She melts into my side, her entire body limp and sated.

"Wow," she finally says, her voice scratchy from all the yelling she just did. I can't help the grin that breaks out on my face, knowing I made her that way. "I mean like…holy shit."

I chuckle and kiss her forehead, pulling her even closer to me. "Yeah," I agree. "I love you so much, Freya. So fucking much," I murmur, tucking some of her sweaty tendrils of hair behind her ear.

"Love you too, Luca. You're more than anything I could have ever hoped for. I never thought…" she sighs and nuzzles her face into the side of my neck. "I never thought I'd get the fairy tale ending, you know?"

I rub calming circles on her back, thinking of how to respond to that. I never thought I'd have it either, but here we are.

"Well, I'm no white knight, and you're no damsel in distress." Freya laughs softly, the sweet sound muffled from where she still has her face buried into my neck. "But you're my happily ever after. You're my forever. My soul. *La mia anima.*"

"You're mine, too. My soul."

I feel her tears on my skin, but I don't make a move. I just hold her and let her feel how perfectly we fit together. How perfectly we complete each other.

Freya fucking Murphy. Who would have guessed the infuriating, gorgeous, brilliant, disaster of a woman would be my whole goddamn world?

Epilogue

Freya

I wake up surrounded by soft blankets and Luca's leather and whiskey scent. I roll over to see if I can wake him up the way I did yesterday morning – with my lips wrapped around his morning wood – but he's not here.

I stretch and take my time getting out of bed before throwing a robe on and wandering out to the kitchen. I pause at the coffee maker, wanting my morning cup, but then smile, remembering why I'll be skipping it for a while. I opt for a glass of orange juice instead, taking it with me as I head to the living room, where I hear Luca talking on the phone to someone.

"What do you mean you lost her *again*? It's been nearly a month!"

He must be talking to Rocco. Poor guy has had a rough go of it lately. I don't know all the details, but apparently, his "simple" job of bringing back a mafia princess isn't so simple after all. If I didn't know better though, I'd think the guy is enjoying the chase.

I can't help the cheesy grin that threatens to split my face in two when I see Luca snuggling on the couch with the Three Stooges. He's barking orders at Rocco while Curly is asleep on his feet, drooling on his socks, no less. Larry is sprawled out on his lap, snoring loudly, and little Mo is snuggled up in the crook of Luca's elbow.

Luca looks up and sees me leaning against the entrance to the living room. The smile that takes over his previously tense features warms me up from the inside out. I did that. I made him smile. I seem to be quite good at it these days.

"Call back when you have more info. If it's not done by the end of the week, I'm sending someone else." Luca doesn't wait for Rocco's response, he just hangs up and tosses his phone aside. "Come here, baby girl. I have something for you."

I skip over to him, feeling light and warm and fuzzy all over. I can't believe this is my life. By the time I get to him, Luca has gently rid himself of the dogs, making space for me on his lap.

"How are you feeling today, *la mia anima*?" He asks, nuzzling the back of my neck and kissing me there. I sigh and melt into his embrace.

"So good," I answer honestly.

I feel his lips pull into a smile against my skin while his hand finds its way to my belly. He can't seem to stop touching me there ever since I told him two days ago that I'm pregnant. He also hasn't stopped doting on me, carrying me around, massaging my feet, feeding me, and otherwise spoiling me. I never thought I'd want a man to take care of me, and I certainly never expected that man to be Luca, but I'm so damn glad I have him.

"That's what I like to hear." Luca sits up a little, adjusting me so I'm sitting sideways on his lap with my legs stretched out to one side.

I can't quite decipher the look he has in his beautiful blue eyes, but he seems nervous about something. I reach out and cup his cheek, rubbing my thumb back and forth over his jaw. Luca leans into my touch, something that will always amaze me. I'm so fucking lucky I get to be the one to see him like this, to hold him like this, to calm him down with my touch. It's humbling and overwhelming in the best way possible.

"You said you had something for me? I like presents," I smile, hoping to ease whatever worried thoughts he has.

Luca nods and digs around in his pocket, producing a gorgeous gold ring with an emerald in the middle and smaller diamonds on the sides. He takes my trembling hand in his and slides the ring on my finger before kissing it and placing my hand back on his cheek.

I'm too shocked to say anything, but I smile through the tears already forming in my eyes, encouraging him to continue.

"I've thought about what to say, how to ask you, for weeks…but nothing is adequate. There are no words big enough to express how much I love you, Freya. I…Jesus, I'm not doing this right," he mutters.

I cup his face in both of my hands and lean down to rest my forehead on his. "I've never done this either, you know. So, whatever you say is still going to be the best proposal I've ever had."

He kisses me, softly, slowly, reverently.

"You're perfect. I never saw you coming, baby girl."

"I find that hard to believe," I tease.

Luca chuckles and kisses the tip of my nose. "You're right. You, Freya Murphy, are hard to miss. I haven't been able to get you out of my head for a single second since the first time I heard your voice on the other end of the phone."

"Not always in a good way though, right?" I wink at him.

"In all the best ways, love. Even when you were pushing all of my buttons, I wanted to know more about you, how you saw the world, what challenges you faced, what made you tick. And when you were pushing me away, all I wanted to know was how I could fight for you, how I could convince you to let me in, let me take care of you. Then when you left…"

God, Luca's eyes fill with unshed tears, which of course, makes me cry all over again. "I'm sorry," I whisper. And I am. I regret all the pain I put both of us through. Darlene, too, and Matteo. Apparently, Leena showed him who's boss, and Matteo readily agreed.

"No more apologies. That's not the point I was trying to make," he reassures me. "I was going to say that when you left, I knew I would stop at nothing to track you down and bring you back. And then when I held you again…fuck, baby girl. I just knew. I knew I wouldn't be complete without you. I know I should have planned something extravagant for this, but I couldn't wait another day without seeing my ring on your finger and knowing you felt the same way."

I nod my head frantically and smile, as tears continue to stream down my face. "I'd really like to say yes now, but you haven't asked me anything yet."

Luca grins and leans in closer, our lips inches apart. He lifts his hand up and trails his fingers down my temple, my cheek, my jaw, my neck, finally resting his hand over my heart. It's become such a familiar, tender gesture between us. A reminder of that first day we kissed, the first day we truly saw each other, felt each other. The first day we knew we shared the same soul.

"Freya, will you challenge me and humble me and bring me to my knees every day for the rest of our lives?"

"Yes," I promise.

"Will you give me all of your pain so that I can share your burden?"

"Yes," I sniffle.

"Will you let me take care of you, of our family, and trust me to protect you always?"

I nod, unable to form even the simplest of answers.

"Will you let me love you, all of you, and give yourself to me? Will you be my best friend, my home, my reason for breathing? Will you be my wife?"

"Yes, yes, yes," I repeat over and over, kissing his face until his laughs and wraps me up in his arms.

"Thank fuck," he breathes out in relief.

I burst out in laughter, which captures the attention of the Three Stooges. Larry and Curly jump up on the couch and burrow their way into my lap, wiggling their cute little butts and licking me and Luca. Mo hops up on the arm of the couch, pretending not to care, but wanting to be a part of the celebration anyway.

"Thank you for giving me everything I've ever wanted but was too scared to hope for," I whisper.

"Funny, I was just going to say the same thing," he grins.

"I don't think that has ever happened!" I gasp dramatically.

Luca pinches my butt, making me squeal. "You're going to be trouble, aren't you?"

I grin at him and nibble his bottom lip. "Yup. And you're going to love every second."

"That I am, baby girl. That I am."

The End

I hope you enjoyed **Loved by the Mafia Underboss**! Please take a moment to leave a review.

Check out the rest of the Moscatelli Crime Family series:
Made for the Mafia Boss
Loved by the Mafia Underboss
Kept by the Mafia Enforcer
Found by the Mafia Capitan

All my love,

Cameron Hart

Made in the USA
Las Vegas, NV
01 March 2021